CLIVE BARKER'S BOOKS OF BLOOD

"He scares even me . . . What Barker does in THE BOOKS OF BLOOD makes the rest of us look like we've been asleep for the last ten years. Some of the stories were so creepily awful that I literally could not read them alone; others go up and over the edge and into gruesome territory . . . He's an original!"
—Stephen King

"Remarkable . . . outstanding . . . Barker is in a class by himself."
—*Locus*

"Original, disturbing, and as discomforting as anything in contemporary literature. This collection heralds the arrival of a major new talent in horror fiction . . . inventive . . . vivid . . . graphic . . . uninhibited mayhem!"
—*Fantasy Review*

"Startling . . . original . . . The most successful of Barker's horror strategies is his ability to pile extraordinary terrors onto ordinary ones . . . a stomach-churning aesthetic."
—*City Limits*

"Barker's visions are at one turn horrifyingly stomach-wrenching and at the next flickering with brilliant invention that leaves the reader shaking . . ."
—*Sounds*

Berkley books by Clive Barker

CLIVE BARKER'S BOOKS OF BLOOD VOLUME I
CLIVE BARKER'S BOOKS OF BLOOD VOLUME II

VOLUME TWO *of* CLIVE BARKER'S

BOOKS *of* BLOOD

BERKLEY BOOKS, NEW YORK

This Berkley book contains the complete
text of the original edition.
It has been completely reset in a typeface
designed for easy reading, and was printed
from new film.

CLIVE BARKER'S BOOKS OF BLOOD VOLUME II

A Berkley Book / published by arrangement with
Sphere Books Limited

PRINTING HISTORY
Sphere Books edition / April 1984
Berkley edition / August 1986

ISBN: 0-425-08739-5

A BERKLEY BOOK ® TM 757,375
Berkley Books are published by The Berkley Publishing Group,
200 Madison Avenue, New York, New York 10016.
The name "BERKLEY" and the stylized "B" with design
are trademarks belonging to Berkley Publishing Corporation.
PRINTED IN THE UNITED STATES OF AMERICA

To Johnny

CONTENTS

Everybody is a book of blood;
wherever we're opened, we're red.

VOLUME TWO of
CLIVE BARKER'S
BOOKS of BLOOD

DREAD

There is no delight the equal of dread. If it were possible to sit, invisible, between two people on any train, in any waiting room or office, the conversation overheard would time and again circle on that subject. Certainly the debate might appear to be about something entirely different; the state of the nation, idle chat about death on the roads, the rising price of dental care; but strip away the metaphor, the innuendo, and there, nestling at the heart of the discourse, is dread. While the nature of God, and the possibility of eternal life go undiscussed, we happily chew over the minutiae of misery. The syndrome recognizes no boundaries; in bath-house and seminar-room alike, the same ritual is repeated. With the inevitability of a tongue returning to probe a painful tooth, we come back and back and back again to our fears, sitting to talk them over with the eagerness of a hungry man before a full and steaming plate.

While he was still at university, and afraid to speak, Stephen Grace was taught to speak of why he was afraid. In fact not simply to talk about it, but to analyze and dissect his every nerve-ending, looking for tiny terrors.

In this investigation, he had a teacher: Quaid.

It was an age of gurus; it was their season. In universities up and down England young men and women were looking east and west for people to follow like lambs; Steve Grace was just one of many. It was his bad luck that Quaid was the Messiah he found.

They'd met in the Student Common Room.

"The name's Quaid," said the man at Steve's elbow at the bar.

"Oh."

"You're—?"

"Steve Grace."

"Yes. You're in the Ethics class, right?"

"Right."

"I don't see you in any of the other Philosophy seminars or lectures."

"It's my extra subject for the year. I'm on the English Literature course. I just couldn't bear the idea of a year in the Old Norse classes."

"So you plumped for Ethics."

"Yes."

Quaid ordered a double brandy. He didn't look that well off, and a double brandy would have just about crippled Steve's finances for the next week. Quaid downed it quickly, and ordered another.

"What are you having?"

Steve was nursing half a pint of luke-warm lager, determined to make it last an hour.

"Nothing for me."

"Yes you will."

"I'm fine."

"Another brandy and a pint of lager for my friend."

Steve didn't resist Quaid's generosity. A pint and a half of lager in his unfed system would help no end in dulling the tedium of his oncoming seminars on "Charles Dickens as a Social Analyst." He yawned just to think of it.

"Somebody ought to write a thesis on drinking as a social activity."

Quaid studied his brandy a moment, then downed it.

"Or as oblivion," he said.

Steve looked at the man. Perhaps five years older than Steve's twenty. The mixture of clothes he wore was confusing. Tattered running shoes, cords, a grey-white shirt that had seen better days: and over it a very expensive black leather jacket that hung badly on his tall, thin frame. The face was long and unremarkable; the eyes milky-blue, and so pale that the color seemed to seep into the whites, leaving just the pin-pricks of his irises visible behind his heavy glasses. Lips full, like a Jagger, but pale, dry and unsensual. Hair, a dirty blond.

Quaid, Steve decided, could have passed for a Dutch dope-pusher.

He wore no badges. They were the common currency of a student's obsessions, and Quaid looked naked without something to imply how he took his pleasures. Was he a gay, feminist, save-the-whale campaigner; or a fascist vegetarian? What was he into, for God's sake?

"You should have been doing Old Norse," said Quaid.

"Why?"

"They don't even bother to mark the papers on that course," said Quaid.

Steve hadn't heard about this. Quaid droned on.

"They just throw them all up into the air. Face up, an A. Face down, a B."

Oh, it was a joke. Quaid was being witty. Steve attempted a laugh, but Quaid's face remained unmoved by his own attempt at humor.

"You should be in Old Norse," he said again. "Who needs Bishop Berkeley anyhow. Or Plato. Or—"

"Or?"

"It's all shit."

"Yes."

"I've watched you, in the Philosophy Class—"

Steve began to wonder about Quaid.

"—You never take notes, do you?"

"No."

"I thought you were either sublimely confident, or you simply couldn't care less."

"Neither. I'm just completely lost."

Quaid grunted, and pulled out a pack of cheap cigarettes. Again, that was not the done thing. You either smoked Gauloises, Camel or nothing at all.

"It's not true philosophy they teach you here," said Quaid, with unmistakable contempt.

"Oh?"

"We get spoonfed a bit of Plato, or a bit of Bentham—no real analysis. It's got all the right markings of course. It looks like the beast: it even smells a bit like the beast to the uninitiated."

"What beast?"

"Philosophy. *True* Philosophy. It's a beast, Stephen. Don't you think?"

"I hadn't—"

"It's wild. It bites."

He grinned, suddenly vulpine.

"Yes. It bites," he replied.

Oh, that pleased him. Again, for luck: "Bites."

Stephen nodded. The metaphor was beyond him.

"I think we should feel mauled by our subject." Quaid was warming to the whole subject of mutilation by education. "We should be frightened to juggle the ideas we should talk about."

"Why?"

"Because if we were philosophers worth we wouldn't be exchanging academic pleasantries. We wouldn't be talking semantics; using linguistic trickery to cover the real concerns."

"What would we be doing?"

Steve was beginning to feel like Quaid's straight-man. Except that Quaid wasn't in a joking mood. His face was set: his pin-prick irises had closed down to tiny dots.

"We should be walking close to the beast, Steve, don't you think? Reaching out to stroke, pet it, milk it—"

"What . . . er . . . what is the beast?"

Quaid was clearly a little exasperated by the pragmatism of the enquiry.

"It's the subject of any worthwhile philosophy, Stephen. It's the things we fear, because we don't understand them. It's the dark behind the door."

Steve thought of a door. Thought of the dark. He began to see what Quaid was driving at in his labyrinthine fashion. Philosophy was a way to talk about fear.

"We should discuss what's intimate to our psyches," said Quaid. "If we don't . . . we risk . . ."

Quaid's loquaciousness deserted him suddenly.

"What?"

Quaid was staring at his empty brandy glass, seeming to will it to be full again.

"Want another?" said Steve, praying that the answer would be no.

"What do we risk?" Quaid repeated the question. "Well, I think if we don't go out and find the beast—"

Steve could see the punchline coming.

"—sooner or later the beast will come and find us."

There is no delight the equal of dread. As long as it's someone else's.

Casually, in the following week or two, Steve made some enquiries about the curious Mr. Quaid.

Nobody knew his first name.

Nobody was certain of his age; but one of the secretaries thought he was over thirty, which came as a surprise.

His parents, Cheryl had heard him say, were dead. Killed, she thought.

That appeared to be the sum of human knowledge where Quaid was concerned.

"I owe you a drink," said Steve, touching Quaid on the shoulder.

He looked as though he'd been bitten.

"Brandy?"

"Thank you."

Steve ordered the drinks.

"Did I startle you?"

"I was thinking."

"No philosopher should be without one."

"One what?"

"Brain."

They fell to talking. Steve didn't know why he'd approached Quaid again. The man was ten years his senior and in a different intellectual league. He probably intimidated Steve, if he was to be honest about it. Quaid's relentless talk of beasts confused him. Yet he wanted more of the same: more metaphors: more of that humorless voice telling him how useless the tutors were, how weak the students.

In Quaid's world there were no certainties. He had no secular gurus and certainly no religion. He seemed incapable of viewing any system, whether it was political or philosophical, without cynicism.

Though he seldom laughed out loud, Steve knew there was a bitter humor in his vision of the world. People were lambs and sheep, all looking for shepherds. Of course these shepherds were fictions, in Quaid's opinion. All that existed, in the darkness outside the sheep-fold, were the fears that fixed on the innocent mutton: waiting, patient as stone, for their moment.

Everything was to be doubted, but the fact that dread existed.

Quaid's intellectual arrogance was exhilarating. Steve soon came to love the iconoclastic ease with which he demolished belief after belief. Sometimes it was painful when Quaid formulated a water-tight argument against one of Steve's dogma. But after a few weeks, even the sound of the demolition seemed to excite. Quaid was clearing the undergrowth, felling the trees, razing the stubble. Steve felt free.

Nation, family, Church, law. All ash. All useless. All

cheats, and chains and suffocation.

There was only dread.

"I fear, you fear, we fear," Quaid was fond of saying. "He, she or it fears. There's no conscious thing on the face of the world that doesn't know dread more intimately than its own heartbeat."

One of Quaid's favorite baiting-victims was another Philosophy and Eng. Lit. student, Cheryl Fromm. She would rise to his more outrageous remarks like fish to rain, and while the two of them took knives to each other's arguments Steve would sit back and watch the spectacle. Cheryl was, in Quaid's phrase, a pathological optimist.

"And you're full of shit," she'd say when the debate had warmed up a little. "So who cares if you're afraid of your own shadow? I'm not. I feel fine."

She certainly looked it. Cheryl Fromm was wet dream material, but too bright for anyone to try making a move on her.

"We all taste dread once in a while," Quaid would reply to her, and his milky eyes would study her face intently, watching for her reaction, trying, Steve knew, to find a flaw in her conviction.

"I don't."

"No fears? No nightmares?"

"No way. I've got a good family; I don't have any skeletons in my closet. I don't even eat meat, so I don't feel bad when I drive past a slaughterhouse. I don't have any shit to put on show. Does that mean I'm not real?"

"It means," Quaid's eyes were snake-slits, "it means your confidence has something big to cover."

"Back to nightmares."

"Big nightmares."

"Be specific: define your terms."

"I can't tell you what you fear."

"Tell me what you fear then."

Quaid hesitated. "Finally," he said, "it's beyond analysis."

"Beyond analysis, my ass!"

That brought an involuntary smile to Steve's lips. Cheryl's ass was indeed beyond analysis. The only response was to kneel down and worship.

Quaid was back on his soap-box.

"What I fear is personal to me. It makes no sense in a larger context. The signs of my dread, the images my brain uses, if you like, to *illustrate* my fear, those signs are mild stuff by comparison with the real horror that's at the root of my personality."

"I've got images," said Steve. "Pictures from childhood that make me think of—" He stopped, regretting this confessional already.

"What?" said Cheryl. "You mean things to do with bad experiences? Falling off your bike, or something like that?"

"Perhaps," Steve said. "I find myself, sometimes, thinking of those pictures. Not deliberately, just when my concentration's idling. It's almost as though my mind went to them automatically."

Quaid gave a little grunt of satisfaction. "Precisely," he said.

"Freud writes on that," said Cheryl.

"What?"

"Freud," Cheryl repeated, this time making a performance of it, as though she were speaking to a child. "Sigmund Freud: you may have heard of him."

Quaid's lip curled with unrestrained contempt. "Mother fixations don't answer the problem. The real terrors in me, in all of us, are pre-personality. Dread's there before we have any notion of ourselves as individuals. The thumb-nail, curled up on itself in the womb, feels fear."

"You remember, do you?" said Cheryl.

"Maybe," Quaid replied, deadly serious.

"The womb?"

Quaid gave a sort of half-smile. Steve thought the smile said: "I have knowledge you don't."

It was a weird, unpleasant smile; one Steve wanted to wash off his eyes.

"You're a liar," said Cheryl, getting up from her seat, and looking down her nose at Quaid.

"Perhaps I am," he said, suddenly the perfect gentleman.

After that the debates stopped.

No more talking about nightmares, no more debating the things that go bump in the night. Steve saw Quaid irregularly for the next month, and when he did Quaid was invariably in the company of Cheryl Fromm. Quaid was polite with her, even deferential. He no longer wore his leather jacket, because she hated the smell of dead animal matter. This sudden change in their relationship confounded Stephen; but he put it down to his primitive understanding of sexual matters. He wasn't a virgin, but women were still a mystery to him: contradictory and puzzling.

He was also jealous, though he wouldn't entirely admit that to himself. He resented the fact that the wet dream genius was taking up so much of Quaid's time.

There was another feeling; a curious sense he had that Quaid was courting Cheryl for his own strange reasons. Sex was not Quaid's motive, he felt sure. Nor was it respect for Cheryl's intelligence that made him so attentive. No, he was cornering her somehow; that was Steve's instinct. Cheryl Fromm was being rounded up for the kill.

Then, after a month, Quaid let a remark about Cheryl drop in conversation.

"She's a vegetarian," he said.

"Cheryl?"

"Of course, Cheryl."

"I know. She mentioned it before."

"Yes, but it isn't a fad with her. She's passionate about it. Can't even bear to look in a butcher's window. She won't touch meat, smell meat—"

"Oh." Steve was stumped. Where was this leading?

"Dread, Steve."

"Of meat?"

"The signs are different from person to person. *She fears meat.* She says she's so healthy, so balanced. Shit! I'll find it—"

"Find what?"

"The fear, Steve."

"You're not going to . . . ?" Steve didn't know how to voice his anxiety without sounding accusatory.

"Harm her?" said Quaid. "No, I'm not going to harm her in any way. Any damage done to her will be strictly self-inflicted."

Quaid was staring at him almost hypnotically.

"It's about time we learned to trust one another," Quaid went on. He leaned closer. "Between the two of us—"

"Listen, I don't think I want to hear."

"We have to touch the beast, Stephen."

"Damn the beast! I don't want to hear!"

Steve got up, as much to break the oppression of Quaid's stare as to finish the conversation.

"We're friends, Stephen."

"Yes . . ."

"Then respect that."

"What?"

"Silence. Not a word."

Steve nodded. That wasn't a difficult promise to keep. There was nobody he could tell his anxieties to without being laughed at.

Quaid looked satisfied. He hurried away, leaving Steve feeling as though he had unwillingly joined some secret society, for what purpose he couldn't begin to tell. Quaid had made a pact with him and it was unnerving.

For the next week he cut all his lectures and most of his seminars. Notes went uncopied, books unread, essays unwritten. On the two occasions he actually went into the university building he crept around like a cautious mouse, praying he wouldn't collide with Quaid.

He needn't have feared. The one occasion he did see Quaid's stooping shoulders across the quadrangle he was involved in a smiling exchange with Cheryl Fromm. She laughed, musically, her pleasure echoing off the wall of the History Department. The jealousy had left Steve altogether. He wouldn't have been paid to be so near to Quaid, so intimate with him.

The time he spent alone, away from the bustle of lectures and overfull corridors, gave Steve's mind time to idle. His thoughts returned, like tongue to tooth, like fingernail to scab, to his fears.

And so to his childhood.

At the age of six, Steve had been struck by a car. The injuries were not particularly bad, but concussion left him partially deaf. It was a profoundly distressing experience for him; not understanding why he was suddenly cut off from the world. It was an inexplicable torment, and the child assumed it was eternal.

One moment his life had been real, full of shouts and laughter. The next he was cut off from it, and the external world became an aquarium, full of gaping fish with grotesque smiles. Worse still, there were times when he suffered what the doctors called tinnitus, a roaring or ringing sound in the ears. His head would fill with the most outlandish noises, whoops and whistlings, that played like sound-effects to the flailings of the outside world. At those times his stomach would churn, and a band of iron would be wrapped around his forehead, crushing his thoughts into fragments, dissociating head from hand, intention from practice. He would be swept away in a tide of panic, completely unable to make sense of the world while his head sang and rattled.

But at night came the worst terrors. He would wake, sometimes, in what had been (before the accident) the reassuring womb of his bedroom, to find the ringing had begun in his sleep.

His eyes would jerk open. His body would be wet with sweat. His mind would be filled with the most raucous din, which he was locked in with, beyond hope of reprieve. Nothing could silence his head, and nothing, it seemed, could bring the world, the speaking, laughing, crying world back to him.

He was alone.

That was the beginning, middle and end of the dread. He was absolutely alone with his cacophony. Locked in this house, in this room, in this body, in this head, a prisoner of deaf, blind flesh.

It was almost unbearable. In the night the boy would sometimes cry out, not knowing he was making any sound, and the fish who had been his parents would turn on the light and come to try and help him, bending over his bed making faces, their soundless mouths forming ugly shapes in their attempts to help. Their touches would calm him at last; with time his mother learned the trick of soothing away the panic that swept over him.

A week before his seventh birthday his hearing returned, not perfectly, but well enough for it to seem like a miracle. The world snapped back into focus; and life began afresh.

It took several months for the boy to trust his senses again. He would still wake in the night, half-anticipating the head-noises.

But though his ears would ring at the slightest volume of sound, preventing Steve from going to rock concerts with the rest of the students, he now scarcely ever noticed his slight deafness.

He remembered, of course. Very well. He could bring back the taste of his panic; the feel of the iron band around his head. And there was a residue of fear there; of the dark, of being alone.

But then, wasn't everyone afraid to be alone? To be utterly alone.

Steve had another fear now, far more difficult to pin down.

Quaid.

In a drunken revelation session he had told Quaid about his childhood, about the deafness, about the night terrors.

Quaid knew about his weakness: the clear route into the heart of Steve's dread. He had a weapon, a stick to beat Steve with, should it ever come to that. Maybe that was why he chose not to speak to Cheryl (warn her, was that what he wanted to do?) and certainly that was why he avoided Quaid.

The man had a look, in certain moods, of malice. Nothing more or less. He looked like a man with malice deep, deep in him.

Maybe those four months of watching people with the sound turned down had sensitized Steve to the tiny glances, sneers and smiles that flit across people's faces. He knew Quaid's life was a labyrinth; a map of its complexities was etched on his face in a thousand tiny expressions.

The next phase of Steve's initiation into Quaid's secret world didn't come for almost three and a half months. The university broke for the summer recess, and the students went their ways. Steve took his usual vacation job at his father's printing works; it was long hours, and physically exhausting, but an undeniable relief for him. Academe had overstuffed his mind, he felt force-fed with words and ideas. The print work sweated all of that out of him rapidly, sorting out the jumble in his mind.

It was a good time: he scarcely thought of Quaid at all.

He returned to campus in the late September. The students were still thin on the ground. Most of the courses didn't start for another week; and there was a melancholy air about the place without its usual mêlée of complaining, flirting, arguing kids.

Steve was in the library, cornering a few important books before others on his course had their hands on them. Books were pure gold at the beginning of term, with reading lists to be checked off, and the university book shop forever claiming the necessary titles were on order. They would invariably arrive, those vital books, two days after the seminar in which the author was to be discussed. This final year Steve was determined to be ahead of the rush for the few copies of seminal works the library possessed.

The familiar voice spoke.

"Early to work."

Steve looked up to meet Quaid's pin-prick eyes.

"I'm impressed, Steve."

"What with?"

"Your enthusiasm for the job."

"Oh."

Quaid smiled. "What are you looking for?"

"Something on Bentham."

"I've got 'Principles of Morals and Legislation.' Will that do?"

It was a trap. No: that was absurd. He was offering a book; how could that simple gesture be construed as a trap?

"Come to think of it," the smile broadened, "I think it's the library copy I've got. I'll give it to you."

"Thanks."

"Good holiday?"

"Yes. Thank you. You?"

"Very rewarding."

The smile had decayed into a thin line beneath his—

"You've grown a moustache."

It was an unhealthy example of the species. Thin, patchy, and dirty-blond, it wandered back and forth under Quaid's nose as if looking for a way off his face. Quaid looked faintly embarrassed.

"Was it for Cheryl?"

He was definitely embarrassed now.

"Well . . ."

"Sounds like you had a good vacation."

The embarrassment was surmounted by something else.

"I've got some wonderful photographs," Quaid said.

"What of?"

"Holiday snaps."

Steve couldn't believe his ears. Had C. Fromm tamed the Quaid? Holiday snaps?

"You won't believe some of them."

There was something of the Arab selling dirty post-cards about Quaid's manner. What the hell were these photographs? Split beaver shots of Cheryl, caught reading Kant?

"I don't think of you as being a photographer."

"It's become a passion of mine."

He grinned as he said "passion." There was a barely-suppressed excitement in his manner. He was positively gleaming with pleasure.

"You've got to come and see them."

"I—"

"Tonight. And pick up the Bentham at the same time."

"Thanks."

"I've got a house for myself these days. Round the corner from the Maternity Hospital, in Pilgrim Street. Number sixty-four. Some time after nine?"

"Right. Thanks. Pilgrim Street."

Quaid nodded.

"I didn't know there were any habitable houses in Pilgrim Street."

"Number sixty-four."

Pilgrim Street was on its knees. Most of the houses were already rubble. A few were in the process of being knocked down. Their inside walls were unnaturally exposed; pink and pale green wallpapers, fireplaces on upper stories hanging over chasms of smoking brick. Stairs leading from nowhere to nowhere, and back again.

Number sixty-four stood on its own. The houses in

the terrace to either side had been demolished and bull-dozed away, leaving a desert of impacted brick-dust which a few hardy, and foolhardy, weeds had tried to populate.

A three-legged white dog was patrolling its territory along the side of sixty-four, leaving little piss-marks at regular intervals as signs of its ownership.

Quaid's house, though scarcely palatial, was more welcoming than the surrounding wasteland.

They drank some bad red wine together, which Steve had brought with him, and they smoked some grass. Quaid was far more mellow than Steve had ever seen him before, quite happy to talk trivia instead of dread; laughing occasionally; even telling a dirty joke. The interior of the house was bare to the point of being spartan. No pictures on the walls; no decoration of any kind. Quaid's books, and there were literally hundreds of them, were piled on the floor in no particular sequence that Steve could make out. The kitchen and bathroom were primitive. The whole atmosphere was almost monastic.

After a couple of easy hours, Steve's curiosity got the better of him.

"Where's the holiday snaps, then?" he said, aware that he was slurring his words a little, and no longer giving a shit.

"Oh yes. My experiment."

"Experiment?"

"Tell you the truth, Steve, I'm not so sure I should show them to you."

"Why not?"

"I'm into serious stuff, Steve."

"And I'm not ready for serious stuff, is that what you're saying?"

Steve could feel Quaid's technique working on him, even though it was transparently obvious what he was doing.

"I didn't say you weren't ready—"

"What the hell is this stuff?"

"Pictures."

"Of?"

"You remember Cheryl."

Pictures of Cheryl. Ha.

"How could I forget?"

"She won't be coming back this term."

"Oh."

"She had a revelation."

Quaid's stare was basilisk-like.

"What do you mean?"

"She was always so calm, wasn't she?" Quaid was talking about her as though she were dead. "Calm, cool, and collected."

"Yes, I suppose she was."

"Poor bitch. All she wanted was a good fuck."

Steve smirked like a kid at Quaid's dirty talk. It was a little shocking; like seeing teacher with his dick hanging out of his trousers.

"She spent some of the vacation here."

"Here?"

"In this house."

"You like her then?"

"She's an ignorant cow. She's pretentious, she's weak, she's stupid. But she wouldn't *give,* she wouldn't give a fucking thing."

"You mean she wouldn't screw?"

"Oh no, she'd strip off her knickers soon as look at you. It was her fears she wouldn't give—"

Same old song.

"But I persuaded her, in the fullness of time."

Quaid pulled out a box from behind a pile of philosophy books. In it was a sheaf of black and white photographs, blown up to twice postcard size. He passed the first one of the series over to Steve.

"I locked her away you see, Steve." Quaid was as unemotional as a newsreader. "To see if I could needle her into showing her dread a little bit."

"What do you mean, locked her away?"

"Upstairs."

Steve felt strange. He could hear his ears singing, very quietly. Bad wine always made his head ring.

"I locked her away upstairs," Quaid said again, "as an experiment. That's why I took this house. No neighbors to hear."

No neighbors to hear what?

Steve looked at the grainy image in his hand.

"Concealed camera," said Quaid, "she never knew I was photographing her."

Photograph One was of a small, featureless room. A little plain furniture.

"That's the room. Top of the house. Warm. A bit stuffy even. No noise."

No noise.

Quaid proffered Photograph Two.

Same room. Now most of the furniture had been removed. A sleeping bag was laid along one wall. A table. A chair. A bare light bulb.

"That's how I laid it out for her."

"It looks like a cell."

Quaid grunted.

Photograph Three. The same room. On the table a jug of water. In the corner of the room, a bucket, roughly covered with a towel.

"What's the bucket for?"

"She had to piss."

"Yes."

"All amenities provided," said Quaid. "I didn't intend to reduce her to an animal."

Even in his drunken state, Steve took Quaid's inference. He didn't *intend* to reduce her to an animal. However . . .

Photograph Four. On the table, on an unpatterned plate, a slab of meat. A bone sticks out from it.

"Beef," said Quaid.

"But she's a vegetarian."

"So she is. It's slightly salted, well-cooked, good beef."

Photograph Five. The same. Cheryl is in the room. The door is closed. She is kicking the door, her foot and fist and face a blur of fury.

"I put her in the room about five in the morning. She was sleeping: I carried her over the threshold myself. Very romantic. She didn't know what the hell was going on."

"You locked her in there?"

"Of course. An experiment."

"She knew nothing about it?"

"We'd talked about dread, you know me. She knew what I wanted to discover. Knew I wanted guinea-pigs. She soon caught on. Once she realized what I was up to she calmed down."

Photograph Six. Cheryl sits in the corner of the room, thinking.

"I think she believed she could out-wait me."

Photograph Seven. Cheryl looks at the leg of beef, glancing at it on the table.

"Nice photo, don't you think? Look at the expression of disgust on her face. She hated even the smell of cooked meat. She wasn't hungry then, of course."

Eight: she sleeps.

Nine: she pisses. Steve felt uncomfortable, watching the girl squatting on the bucket, knickers round her ankles. Tearstains on her face.

Ten: she drinks water from the jug.

Eleven: she sleeps again, back to the room, curled up like a fetus.

"How long has she been in the room?"

"This was only fourteen hours in. She lost orientation as to time very quickly. No light change, you see. Her body-clock was fucked up pretty soon."

"How long was she in here?"

"Till the point was proved."

Twelve: Awake, she cruises the meat on the table,

caught surreptitiously glancing down at it.

"This was taken the following morning. I was asleep: the camera just took pictures every quarter hour. Look at her eyes . . ."

Steve peered more closely at the photograph. There was a certain desperation on Cheryl's face: a haggard, wild look. The way she stared at the beef she could have been trying to hypnotize it.

"She looks sick."

"She's tired, that's all. She slept a lot, as it happened, but it seemed just to make her more exhausted than ever. She doesn't know now if it's day or night. And she's hungry of course. It's been a day and a half. She's more than a little peckish."

Thirteen: she sleeps again, curled into an even tighter ball, as though she wanted to swallow herself.

Fourteen: she drinks more water.

"I replaced the jug when she was asleep. She slept deeply: I could have done a jig in there and it wouldn't have woken her. Lost to the world."

He grinned. Mad, thought Steve, the man's mad.

"God, it stank in there. You know how women smell sometimes; it's not sweat, it's something else. Heavy odor: meaty. Bloody. She came on towards the end of her time. Hadn't planned it that way."

Fifteen: she touches the meat.

"This is where the cracks begin to show," said Quaid, with quiet triumph in his voice. "This is where the dread begins."

Steve studied the photograph closely. The grain of the print blurred the detail, but the cool mama was in pain, that was for sure. Her face was knotted up, half in desire, half in repulsion, as she touched the food.

Sixteen: she was at the door again, throwing herself at it, every part of her body flailing. Her mouth a black blur of angst, screaming at the blank door.

"She always ended up haranguing me, whenever she'd had a confrontation with the meat."

"How long is this?"

"Coming up for three days. You're looking at a hungry woman."

It wasn't difficult to see that. The next photo she stood still in the middle of the room, averting her eyes from the temptation of the food, her entire body tensed with the dilemma.

"You're starving her."

"She can go ten days without eating quite easily. Fasts are common in any civilized country, Steve. Sixty percent of the British population is clinically obese at any one time. She was too fat anyhow."

Eighteen: she sits, the fat girl, in her corner of the room, weeping.

"About now she began to hallucinate. Just little mental ticks. She thought she felt something in her hair, or on the back of her hand. I'd see her staring into mid-air sometimes watching nothing."

Nineteen: she washes herself. She is stripped to the waist, her breasts are heavy, her face is drained of expression. The meat is a darker tone than in the previous photographs.

"She washed herself regularly. Never let twelve hours go by without washing from head to toe."

"The meat looks . . ."

"Ripe?"

"Dark."

"It's quite warm in her little room; and there's a few flies in there with her. They've found the meat: laid their eggs. Yes, it's ripening up quite nicely."

"Is that part of the plan?"

"Sure. If the meat revolted when it was fresh, what about her disgust at rotted meat? That's the crux of her dilemma, isn't it? The longer she waits to eat, the more disgusted she becomes with what she's been given to feed on. She's trapped with her own horror of meat on the one hand, and her dread of dying on the other. Which is going to give first?"

Steve was no less trapped now.

On the one hand this joke had already gone too far, and Quaid's experiment had become an exercise in sadism. On the other hand he wanted to know how far this story ended. There was an undeniable fascination in watching the woman suffer.

The next seven photographs—twenty, twenty-one, two, three, four, five and six pictured the same circular routine. Sleeping, washing, pissing, meat-watching. Sleeping, washing, pissing—

Then twenty-seven.

"See?"

She picks up the meat.

Yes, she picks it up, her face full of horror. The haunch of the beef looks well-ripened now, speckled with flies' eggs. Gross.

"She bites it."

The next photograph, and her face is buried in the meat.

Steve seemed to taste the rotten flesh in the back of his throat. His mind found a stench to imagine, and created a gravy of putresence to run over his tongue. How could she do it?

Twenty-nine: she is vomiting in the bucket in the corner of the room.

Thirty: she is sitting looking at the table. It is empty. The water-jug has been thrown against the wall. The plate has been smashed. The beef lies on the floor in a slime of degeneration.

Thirty-one: she sleeps. Her head is lost in a tangle of arms.

Thirty-two: she is standing up. She is looking at the meat again, defying it. The hunger she feels is plain on her face. So is the disgust.

Thirty-three. She sleeps.

"How long now?" asked Steve.

"Five days. No, six."

Six days.

Thirty-four. She is a blurred figure, apparently flinging herself against a wall. Perhaps beating her head against it, Steve couldn't be sure. He was past asking. Part of him didn't want to know.

Thirty-five: she is again sleeping, this time beneath the table. The sleeping bag has been torn to pieces, shredded cloth and pieces of stuffing littering the room.

Thirty-six: she speaks to the door, through the door, knowing she will get no answer.

Thirty-seven: she eats the rancid meat.

Calmly she sits under the table, like a primitive in her cave, and pulls at the meat with her incisors. Her face is again expressionless; all her energy is bent to the purpose of the moment. To eat. To eat 'til the hunger disappears, 'til the agony in her belly, and the sickness in her head disappear.

Steve stared at the photograph.

"It startled me," said Quaid, "how suddenly she gave in. One moment she seemed to have as much resistance as ever. The monologue at the door was the same mixture of threats and apologies as she'd delivered day in, day out. Then she broke. Just like that. Squatted under the table and ate the beef down to the bone, as though it were a choice cut."

Thirty-eight: she sleeps. The door is open. Light pours in.

Thirty-nine: the room is empty.

"Where did she go?"

"She wandered downstairs. She came into the kitchen, drank several glasses of water, and sat in a chair for three or four hours without saying a word."

"Did you speak to her?"

"Eventually. When she started to come out of her fugue state. The experiment was over. I didn't want to hurt her."

"What did she say?"

"Nothing."

"Nothing?"

"Nothing at all. For a long time I don't believe she was even aware of my presence in the room. Then I cooked some potatoes, which she ate."

"She didn't try and call the police?"

"No."

"No violence?"

"No. She knew what I'd done, and why I'd done it. It wasn't pre-planned, but we'd talked about such experiments, in abstract conversations. She hadn't come to any harm, you see. She'd lost a bit of weight perhaps, but that was about all."

"Where is she now?"

"She left the day after. I don't know where she went."

"And what did it all prove?"

"Nothing at all, perhaps. But it made an interesting start to my investigations."

"Start? This was only a start?"

There was plain disgust for Quaid in Steve's voice.

"Stephen—"

"You could have killed her!"

"No."

"She could have lost her mind. Unbalanced her permanently."

"Possibly. But unlikely. She was a strong-willed woman."

"But you broke her."

"Yes. It was a journey she was ready to take. We'd talked of going to face her fear. So here was I, arranging for Cheryl to do just that. Nothing much really."

"You forced her to do it. She wouldn't have gone otherwise."

"True. It was an education for her."

"So now you're a teacher?"

Steve wished he'd been able to keep the sarcasm out of his voice. But it was there. Sarcasm; anger; and a little fear.

"Yes, I'm a teacher," Quaid replied, looking at Steve

obliquely, his eyes not focussed. "I'm teaching people dread."

Steve stared at the floor. "Are you satisfied with what you've taught?"

"And learned, Steve. I've learned too. It's a very exciting prospect: a world of fears to investigate. Especially with intelligent subjects. Even in the face of rationalization—"

Steve stood up. "I don't want to hear any more."

"Oh? OK."

"I've got classes early tomorrow."

"No."

"What?"

A beat, faltering.

"No. Don't go yet."

"Why?" His heart was racing. He feared Quaid, he'd never realized how profoundly.

"I've got some more books to give you."

Steve felt his face flush. Slightly. What had he thought in that moment? That Quaid was going to bring him down with a rugby tackle and start experimenting on his fears?

No. Idiot thoughts.

"I've got a book on Kierkegaard you'll like. Upstairs. I'll be two minutes."

Smiling, Quaid left the room.

Steve squatted on his haunches and began to sheaf through the photographs again. It was the moment when Cheryl first picked up the rotting meat that fascinated him most. Her face wore an expression completely uncharacteristic of the woman he had known. Doubt was written there, and confusion, and deep—

Dread.

It was Quaid's word. A dirty word. An obscene word, associated from this night on with Quaid's torture of an innocent girl.

For a moment Steve thought of the expression on his own face, as he stared down at the photograph. Was

there not some of the same confusion on his face? And
perhaps some of the dread too, waiting for release.

He heard a sound behind him, too soft to be Quaid.

Unless he was creeping.

Oh, God, unless he was—

A pad of chloroformed cloth was clamped over
Steve's mouth and his nostrils. Involuntarily, he inhaled
and the vapors stung his sinuses, made his eyes water.

A blob of blackness appeared at the corner of the
world, just out of sight, and it started to grow, this
stain, pulsing to the rhythm of his quickening heart.

In the center of Steve's head he could see Quaid's
voice as a veil. It said his name.

"Stephen."

Again.

"—ephen."

"—phen."

"—hen."

"en."

The stain was the world. The world was dark, gone
away. Out of sight, out of mind.

Steve fell clumsily amongst the photographs.

When he woke up he was unaware of his consciousness.
There was darkness everywhere, on all sides. He lay
awake for an hour with his eyes wide before he realized
they were open.

Experimentally, he moved first his arms and his legs,
then his head. He wasn't bound as he'd expected, except
by his ankle. There was definitely a chain or something
similar around his left ankle. It chafed his skin when he
tried to move too far.

The floor beneath him was very uncomfortable, and
when he investigated it more closely with the palm of his
hand he realized he was lying on a huge grille or grid of
some kind. It was metal, and its regular surface spread
in every direction as far as his arms would reach. When
he poked his arm down through the holes in this lattice

he touched nothing. Just empty air falling away beneath him.

The first infra-red photographs Quaid took of Stephen's confinement pictured his exploration. As Quaid had expected the subject was being quite rational about his situation. No hysterics. No curses. No tears. That was the challenge of this particular subject. He knew precisely what was going on; and he would respond logically to his fears. That would surely make a more difficult mind to break than Cheryl's.

But how much more rewarding the results would be when he did crack. Would his soul not open up then, for Quaid to see and touch? There was so much there, in the man's interior, he wanted to study.

Gradually Steve's eyes became accustomed to the darkness.

He was imprisoned in what appeared to be some kind of shaft. It was, he estimated, about twenty feet wide, and completely round. Was it some kind of air-shaft, for a tunnel, or an underground factory? Steve's mind mapped the area around Pilgrim Street, trying to pinpoint the most likely place for Quaid to have taken him. He could think of nowhere.

Nowhere.

He was lost in a place he couldn't fix or recognize. The shaft had no corners to focus his eyes on; and the walls offered no crack or hole to hide his consciousness in.

Worse, he was lying spreadeagled on a grid that hung over this shaft. His eyes could make no impression on the darkness beneath him: it seemed that the shaft might be bottomless. And there was only the thin network of the grille, and the fragile chain that shackled his ankle to it, between him and falling.

He pictured himself poised under an empty black sky, and over an infinite darkness. The air was warm and stale. It dried up the tears that had suddenly sprung to

his eyes, leaving them gummy. When he began to shout
for help, which he did after the tears had passed, the
darkness ate his words easily.

Having yelled himself hoarse, he lay back on the lattice. He couldn't help but imagine that beyond his frail
bed, the darkness went on forever. It was absurd, of
course. Nothing goes on forever, he said aloud.

Nothing goes on forever.

And yet, he'd never know. If he fell in the absolute
blackness beneath him, he'd fall and fall and fall and
not see the bottom of the shaft coming. Though he tried
to think of brighter, more positive, images, his mind
conjured his body cascading down this horrible shaft,
with the bottom a foot from his hurtling body and his
eyes not seeing it, his brain not predicting it.

Until he hit.

Would he see light as his head was dashed open on
impact? Would he understand, in the moment that his
body became offal, why he'd lived and died?

Then he thought: Quaid wouldn't dare. "Wouldn't
dare!" he screeched. "Wouldn't dare!"

The dark was a glutton for words. As soon as he'd
yelled into it, it was as though he'd never made a sound.

And then another thought: a real baddie. Suppose
Quaid had found this circular hell to put him in because
it would *never* be found, *never* be investigated? Maybe
he wanted to take his experiment to the limits.

To the limits. Death was at the limits. And wouldn't
that be the ultimate experiment for Quaid? Watching a
man die: watching the fear of death, the motherlode of
dread, approach. Sartre had written that no man could
ever know his own death. But to know the deaths of
others, intimately—to watch the acrobatics that the
mind would surely perform to avoid the bitter truth—
that was a clue to death's nature, wasn't it? That might,
in some small way, prepare a man for his own death. To
live another's dread vicariously was the safest, cleverest
way to touch the beast.

Yes, he thought, Quaid might kill me; out of his own terror.

Steve took a sour satisfaction in that thought. That Quaid, the impartial experimenter, the would-be educator, was obsessed with terrors because his own dread ran deepest.

That was why he had to watch others deal with their fears. He needed a solution, a way out for himself.

Thinking all this through took hours. In the darkness Steve's mind was quick-silver, but uncontrollable. He found it difficult to keep one train of argument for very long. His thoughts were like fish, small, fast fish, wriggling out of his grasp as soon as he took a hold of them.

But underlying every twist of thought was the knowledge that he must out-play Quaid. That was certain. He must be calm; prove himself a useless subject for Quaid's analysis.

The photographs of these hours showed Stephen lying with his eyes closed on the grid, with a slight frown on his face. Occasionally, paradoxically, a smile would flit across his lips. Sometimes it was impossible to know if he was sleeping or waking, thinking or dreaming.

Quaid waited.

Eventually Steve's eyes began to flicker under his lids, the unmistakable sign of dreaming. It was time, while the subject slept, to turn the wheel of the rack—

Steve woke with his hands cuffed together. He could see a bowl of water on a plate beside him; and a second bowl, full of luke-warm unsalted porridge, beside it. He ate and drank thankfully.

As he ate, two things registered. First, that the noise of his eating seemed very loud in his head; and second, that he felt a construction, a tightness, around his temples.

The photographs show Stephen clumsily reaching up to his head. A harness is strapped on to him, and locked in place. It clamps plugs deep into his ears, preventing any sound from getting in.

The photographs show puzzlement. Then anger. Then fear.

Steve was deaf.

All he could hear were the noises in his head. The clicking of his teeth. The slush and swallow of his palate. The sounds boomed between his ears like guns.

Tears sprang to his eyes. He kicked at the grid, not hearing the clatter of his heels on the metal bars. He screamed until his throat felt as if it was bleeding. He heard none of his cries.

Panic began in him.

The photographs showed its birth. His face was flushed. His eyes were wide, his teeth and gums exposed in a grimace.

He looked like a frightened monkey.

All the familiar, childhood feelings swept over him. He remembered them like the faces of old enemies; the chittering limbs, the sweat, the nausea. In desperation he picked up the bowl of water and upturned it over his face. The shock of the cold water diverted his mind momentarily from the panic-ladder it was climbing. He lay back down on the grid, his body a board, and told himself to breathe deeply and evenly.

Relax, relax, relax, he said aloud.

In his head, he could hear his tongue clicking. He could hear his mucus too, moving sluggishly in the panic-constricted passages of his nose, blocking and unblocking in his ears. Now he could detect the low, soft hiss that waited under all the other noises. The sound of his mind—

It was like the white noise between stations on the radio, this was the same whine that came to fetch him under anesthetic, the same noise that would sound in his ears on the borders of sleep.

His limbs still twitched nervously, and he was only half-aware of the way he wrestled with his handcuffs, indifferent to their edges scouring the skin at his wrists.

The photographs recorded all these reactions precisely. His war with hysteria: his pathetic attempts to keep the fears from resurfacing. His tears. His bloody wrists.

Eventually, exhaustion won over panic; as it had so often as a child. How many times had he fallen asleep with the salt-taste of tears in his nose and mouth, unable to fight any longer?

The exertion had heightened the pitch of his head-noises. Now, instead of a lullaby, his brain whistled and whooped him to sleep.

Oblivion was good.

Quaid was disappointed. It was clear from the speed of his response that Stephen Grace was going to break very soon indeed. In fact, he was as good as broken, only a few hours into the experiment. And Quaid had been relying on Stephen. After months of preparing the ground, it seemed that this subject was going to lose his mind without giving up a single clue.

One word, one miserable word was all Quaid needed. A little sign as to the nature of the experience. Or better still, something to suggest a solution, a healing totem, a prayer even. Surely some Savior comes to the lips, as the personality is swept away in madness? There must be *something*.

Quaid waited like a carrion bird at the site of some atrocity, counting the minutes left to the expiring soul, hoping for a morsel.

Steve woke face down on the grid. The air was much staler now, and the metal bars bit into the flesh of his cheek. He was hot and uncomfortable.

He lay still, letting his eyes become accustomed to his surroundings again. The lines of the grid ran off in perfect perspective to meet the wall of the shaft. The simple network of criss-crossed bars struck him as pretty. Yes, pretty. He traced the lines back and forth, 'til he tired of the game. Bored, he rolled over onto his back, feeling the grid vibrate under his body. Was it less stable now?

It seemed to rock a little as he moved.

Hot and sweaty, Steve unbuttoned his shirt. There was sleep-spittle on his chin but he didn't care to wipe it off. What if he drooled? Who was to see?

He half pulled off his shirt, and using one foot, kicked his shoe off the other.

Shoe: lattice: fall. Sluggishly, his mind made the connection. He sat up. Oh poor shoe. His shoe would fall. It would slip between the bars and be lost. But no. It was finely balanced across two sides of a lattice-hole; he could still save it if he tried.

He reached for his poor, poor shoe, and his movement shifted the grid.

The shoe began to slip.

"Please," he begged it, "don't fall." He didn't want to lose his nice shoe, his pretty shoe. It mustn't fall. It mustn't fall.

As he stretched to snatch it, the shoe tipped, heel down, through the grid and fell into the darkness.

He let out a cry of loss that he couldn't hear.

Oh, if only he could listen to the shoe falling; to count the seconds of its descent. To hear it thud home at the bottom of the shaft. At least then he'd know how far he had to fall to his death.

He couldn't endure it any longer. He rolled over on to his stomach and thrust both arms through the grid, screaming:

"I'll go too! I'll go too!"

He couldn't bear waiting to fall, in the dark, in the whining silence, he just wanted to follow his shoe down, down, down the dark shaft to extinction, and have the whole game finished once and for all.

"I'll go! I'll go! I'll go!" he shrieked. He pleaded with gravity.

Beneath him, the grid moved.

Something had broken. A pin, a chain, a rope that held the grid in position had snapped. He was no longer horizontal; already he was sliding across the bars as they tipped him off into the dark.

With shock he realized his limbs were no longer chained.

He would fall.

The man wanted him to fall. The bad man—what was his name? Quake? Quail? Quarrel—

Automatically he seized the grid with both hands as it tipped even further over. Maybe he didn't want to fall after his shoe, after all? Maybe life, a little moment more of life, was worth holding on to—

The dark beyond the edge of the grid was so deep; and who could guess what lurked in it?

In his head the noises of his panic multiplied. The thumping of his bloody heart, the stutter of his mucus, the dry rasp of his palate. His palms, slick with sweat, were losing their grip. Gravity wanted him. It demanded its rights of his body's bulk: demanded that he fall. For a moment, glancing over his shoulder at the mouth that opened under him, he thought he saw monsters stirring below him. Ridiculous, loony things, crudely drawn, dark on dark. Vile graffiti leered up from his childhood and uncurled their claws to snatch at his legs.

"Mama," he said, as his hands failed him, and he was delivered into dread.

"Mama."

That was the word. Quaid heard it plainly, in all its banality.

"Mama!"

By the time Steve hit the bottom of the shaft, he was past judging how far he'd fallen. The moment his hands let go of the grid, and he knew the dark would have him, his mind snapped. The animal self survived to relax his body, saving him all but minor injury on impact. The rest of his life, all but the simplest responses, were shattered, the pieces flung into the recesses of his memory.

When the light came, at last, he looked up at the person in the Mickey Mouse mask at the door, and smiled at him. It was a child's smile, one of thankfulness for his comical rescuer. He let the man take him by the ankles and haul him out of the big round room in which he was lying. His pants were wet, and he knew he'd dirtied himself in his sleep. Still, the Funny Mouse would kiss him better.

His head lolled on his shoulders as he was dragged out of the torture-chamber. On the floor beside his head was a shoe. And seven or eight feet above him was the grid from which he had fallen.

It meant nothing at all.

He let the Mouse sit him down in a bright room. He let the Mouse give him his ears back, though he didn't really want them. It was funny watching the world without sound, it made him laugh.

He drank some water, and ate some sweet cake.

He was tired. He wanted to sleep. He wanted his Mama. But the Mouse didn't seem to understand, so he cried, and kicked the table and threw the plates and cups on the floor. Then he ran into the next room, and threw all the papers he could find in the air. It was nice watching them flutter up and flutter down. Some of them fell face down, some face up. Some were covered with writing. Some were pictures. Horrid pictures. Pictures that made him feel very strange.

They were all pictures of dead people, every one of them. Some of the pictures were of little children, others were of grown-up children. They were lying down, or half-sitting, and there were big cuts in their faces and their bodies, cuts that showed a mess underneath, a mish-mash of shiny bits and oozy bits. And all around the dead people: black paint. Not in neat puddles, but splashed all around, and finger-marked, and hand-printed and very messy.

In three or four of the pictures the thing that made the cuts was still there. He knew the word for it.

Axe.

There was an axe in a lady's face buried almost to the handle. There was an axe in a man's leg, and another lying on the floor of a kitchen beside a dead baby.

This man collected pictures of dead people and axes,

which Stevie thought was strange.

That was his last thought before the too-familiar scent of chloroform filled his head and he lost consciousness.

The sordid doorway smelt of old urine and fresh vomit. It was his own vomit; it was all over the front of his shirt. He tried to stand up, but his legs felt wobbly. It was very cold. His throat hurt.

Then he heard footsteps. It sounded like the Mouse was coming back. Maybe he'd take him home.

"Get up, son."

It wasn't the Mouse. It was a policeman.

"What are you doing down there? I said get up."

Bracing himself against the crumbling brick of the doorway Steve got to his feet. The policeman shone his torch at him.

"Jesus Christ," said the policeman, disgust written over his face. "You're in a right fucking state. Where do you live?"

Steve shook his head, staring down at his vomit-soaked shirt like a shamed schoolboy.

"What's your name?"

He couldn't quite remember.

"Name, lad?"

He was trying. If only the policeman wouldn't shout.

"Come on, take a hold of yourself."

The words didn't make much sense. Steve could feel tears pricking the backs of his eyes.

"Home."

Now he was blubbering, sniffing snot, feeling utterly forsaken. He wanted to die: he wanted to lie down and die.

The policeman shook him.

"You high on something?" he demanded, pulling Steve into the glare of the streetlights and staring at his tear-stained face.

"You'd better move on."

"Mama," said Steve, "I want my Mama."

The words changed the encounter entirely.

Suddenly the policeman found the spectacle more than disgusting; more than pitiful. This little bastard, with his bloodshot eyes and his dinner down his shirt, was really getting on his nerves. Too much money, too much dirt in his veins, too little discipline.

"Mama" was the last straw. He punched Steve in the stomach, a neat, sharp, functional blow. Steve doubled up, whimpering.

"Shut up, son."

Another blow finished the job of crippling the child, and then he took a fistful of Steve's hair and pulled the little druggy's face up to meet his.

"You want to be a derelict, is that it?"

"No. No."

Steve didn't know what a derelict was; he just wanted to make the policeman like him.

"Please," he said, tears coming again, "take me home."

The policeman seemed confused. The kid hadn't started fighting back and calling for civil rights, the way most of them did. That was the way they usually ended up: on the ground, bloody-nosed, calling for a social worker. This one just wept. The policeman began to get a bad feeling about the kid. Like he was mental or something. And he'd beaten the shit out of the little snot. Fuck it. Now he felt responsible. He took hold of Steve by the arm and bundled him across the road to his car.

"Get in."

"Take me—"

"I'll take you home, son. I'll take you home."

At the Night Hostel they searched Steve's clothes for some kind of identification, found none, then scoured his body for fleas, his hair for nits. The policeman left him then, which Steve was relieved about. He hadn't liked the man.

The people at the Hostel talked about him as though he wasn't in the room. Talked about how young he was; discussed his mental-age; his clothes; his appearance. Then they gave him a bar of soap and showed him the showers. He stood under the cold water for ten minutes and dried himself with a stained towel. He didn't shave, though they'd lent him a razor. He'd forgotten how to do it.

Then they gave him some old clothes, which he liked. They weren't such bad people, even if they did talk about him as though he wasn't there. One of them even smiled at him; a burly man with a grizzled beard. Smiled as he would at a dog.

They were odd clothes he was given. Either too big or too small. All colors: yellow socks, dirty white shirt, pin-stripe trousers that had been made for a glutton, a thread-bare sweater, heavy boots. He liked dressing up, putting on two vests and two pairs of socks when they weren't looking. He felt assured with several thicknesses of cotton and wool wrapped around him.

Then they left him with a ticket for his bed in his hand, to wait for the dormitories to be unlocked. He was not impatient, like some of the men in the corridors with him. They yelled incoherently, many of them, their accusations laced with obscenities, and they spat at each other. It frightened him. All he wanted was to sleep. To lie down and sleep.

At eleven o'clock one of the warders unlocked the gate to the dormitory, and all the lost men filed through to find themselves an iron bed for the night. The dormitory, which was large and badly lit, stank of disinfectant and old people.

Avoiding the eyes and the flailing arms of the other derelicts, Steve found himself an ill-made bed, with one thin blanket tossed across it, and lay down to sleep. All around him men were coughing and muttering and weeping. One was saying his prayers as he lay, staring at the ceiling, on his grey pillow. Steve thought that was a good idea. So he said his own child's prayer.

"Gentle Jesus, meek and mild,
Look upon this little child,
Pity my—
What was the word?
Pity my—*simplicity*,
Suffer me to come to thee."
That made him feel better; and the sleep, a balm, was
blue and deep.

Quaid sat in darkness. The terror was on him again,
worse than ever. His body was rigid with fear; so much
so that he couldn't even get out of bed and snap on the
light. Besides, what if this time, this time of all times, the
terror was true? What if the axe-man was at the door in
flesh and blood? Grinning like a loon at him, dancing
like the devil at the top of the stairs, as Quaid had seen
him, in dreams, dancing and grinning, grinning and
dancing.

Nothing moved. No creak of the stair, no giggle in the
shadows. It wasn't him, after all. Quaid would live 'til
morning.

His body had relaxed a little now. He swung his legs
out of bed and switched on the light. The room was indeed empty. The house was silent. Through the open
door he could see the top of the stairs. There was no
axe-man, of course.

Steve woke to shouting. It was still dark. He didn't
know how long he'd been asleep, but his limbs no longer
ached so badly. Elbows on his pillow, he half-sat up and
stared down the dormitory to see what all the commo-
tion was about. Four bed-rows down from his, two men
were fighting. The bone of contention was by no means
clear. They just grappled with each other like girls (it
made Steve laugh to watch them), screeching and pulling each other's hair. By moonlight the blood on their
faces and hands was black: One of them, the older of
the two, was thrust back across his bed, screaming: "I

will not go to the Finchley Road! You will not make me. Don't strike me! I'm not your man! I'm not!''

The other was beyond listening; he was too stupid, or too mad, to understand that the old man was begging to be left alone. Urged on by spectators on every side, the old man's assailant had taken off his shoe and was belaboring his victim with it. Steve could hear the crack, crack of his blows: heel on head. There were cheers accompanying each strike, and lessening cries from the old man.

Suddenly, the applause faltered, as somebody came into the dormitory. Steve couldn't see who it was; the mass of men crowded around the fight were between him and the door.

He did see the victor toss his shoe into the air however, with a final shout of ''Fucker!''

The shoe.

Steve couldn't take his eyes off the shoe. It rose in the air, turning as it rose, then plummeted to the bare boards like a shot bird. Steve saw it clearly, more clearly than he'd seen anything in many days.

It landed not far from him.

It landed with a loud thud.

It landed on its side. As his shoe had landed. His shoe. The one he kicked off. On the grid. In the room. In the house. In Pilgrim Street.

Quaid woke with the same dream. Always the stairway. Always him looking down the tunnel of the stairs, while that ridiculous sight, half-joke, half-horror, tip-toed up towards him, a laugh on every step.

He'd never dreamt twice in one night before. He swung his hand out over the edge of the bed and fumbled for the bottle he kept there. In the dark he swigged from it, deeply.

Steve walked past the knot of angry men, not caring about their shouts or the old man's groans and curses.

The warders were having a hard time dealing with the disturbance. It was the last time Old Man Crowley would be let in: he always invited violence. This had all the marks of a near-riot; it would take hours to settle them down again.

Nobody questioned Steve as he wandered down the corridor, through the gate, and into the vestibule of the Night Hostel. The swing doors were closed, but the night air, bitter before dawn, smelt refreshing as it seeped in.

The pokey reception office was empty, and through the door Steve could see the fire-extinguisher hanging on the wall. It was red and bright. Beside it was a long black hose, curled up on a red drum like a sleeping snake. Beside that, sitting in two brackets on the wall, was an axe.

A very pretty axe.

Stephen walked into the office. A little distance away he heard running feet, shouts, a whistle. But nobody came to interrupt Steve, as he made friends with the axe.

First he smiled at it.

The curve of the blade of the axe smiled back.

Then he touched it.

The axe seemed to like being touched. It was dusty, and hadn't been used in a long while. Too long. It wanted to be picked up, and stroked, and smiled at. Steve took it out of its brackets very gently, and slid it under his jacket to keep warm. Then he walked back out of the reception office, through the swing-doors and out to find his other shoe.

Quaid woke again.

It took Steve a very short time to orient himself. There was a spring in his step as he began to make his way to Pilgrim Street. He felt like a clown, dressed in so many bright colors, in such floppy trousers, such silly boots. He was a comical fellow, wasn't he? He made himself laugh, he was so comical.

The wind began to get into him, whipping him up into a frenzy as it scooted through his hair and made his eyeballs as cold as two lumps of ice in his sockets.

He began to run, skip, dance, cavort through the streets, white under the lights, dark in between. Now you see me, now you don't. Now you see me, now you—

Quaid hadn't been woken by the dream this time. This time he had heard a noise. Definitely a noise.

The moon had risen high enough to throw its beams through the window, through the door and on to the top of the stairs. There was no need to put on the light. All he needed to see, he could see. The top of the stairs were empty, as ever.

Then the bottom stair creaked, a tiny noise as though a breath had landed on it.

Quaid knew dread then.

Another creak, as it came up the stairs towards him, the ridiculous dream. It had to be a dream. After all, he knew no clowns, no axe-killers. So how could that absurd image, the same image that woke him night after night, be anything but a dream?

Yet, perhaps there were some dreams so preposterous they could only be true.

No clowns, he said to himself, as he stood watching the door, and the stairway, and the spotlight of the moon. Quaid knew only fragile minds, so weak they couldn't give him a clue to the nature, to the origin, or to the cure for the panic that now held him in thrall. All they did was break, crumble into dust, when faced with the slightest sign of the dread at the heart of life.

He knew no clowns, never had, never would.

Then it appeared; the face of a fool. Pale to whiteness in the light of the moon, its young features bruised, unshaven and puffy, its smile open like a child's smile. It had bitten its lip in its excitement. Blood was smeared across it lower jaw, and its gums were almost black with blood. Still it was a clown. Indisputably a clown even to its ill-fitting clothes, so incongruous, so pathetic.

Only the axe didn't quite match the smile.

It caught the moonlight as the maniac made small, chopping motions with it, his tiny black eyes glinting with anticipation of the fun ahead.

Almost at the top of the stairs, he stopped, his smile not faltering for a moment as he gazed at Quaid's terror.

Quaid's legs gave out, and he stumbled to his knees.

The clown climbed another stair, skipping as he did so, his glittering eyes fixed on Quaid, filled with a sort of benign malice. The axe rocked back and forth in his white hands, in a petite version of the killing stroke.

Quaid knew him.

It was his pupil: his guinea-pig, transformed into the image of his own dread.

Him. Of all men. Him. The deaf boy.

The skipping was bigger now, and the clown was making a deep-throated noise, like the call of some fantastical bird. The axe was describing wider and wider sweeps in the air, each more lethal than the last.

"Stephen," said Quaid.

The name meant nothing to Steve. All he saw was the mouth opening. The mouth closing. Perhaps a sound came out: perhaps not. It was irrelevant to him.

The throat of the clown gave out a screech, and the axe swung up over his head, two-handed. At the same moment the merry little dance became a run, as the axe-man leapt the last two stairs and ran into the bedroom, full into the spotlight.

Quaid's body half turned to avoid the killing blow, but not quickly or elegantly enough. The blade slit the air and sliced through the back of Quaid's arm, sheering off most of his triceps, shattering his humerus and opening the flesh of his lower arm in a gash that just missed his artery.

Quaid's scream could have been heard ten houses away, except that those houses were rubble. There was nobody to hear. Nobody to come and drag the clown off him.

The axe, eager to be about its business, was hacking at Quaid's thigh now, as though it was chopping a log. Yawning wounds four or five inches deep exposed the shiny steak of the philosopher's muscle, the bone, the marrow. With each stroke the clown would tug at the axe to pull it out, and Quaid's body would jerk like a puppet.

Quaid screamed. Quaid begged. Quaid cajoled.

The clown didn't hear a word.

All he heard was the noise in his head: the whistles, the whoops, the howls, the hums. He had taken refuge where no rational argument, no threat, would ever fetch him out again. Where the thump of his heart was law, and the whine of his blood was music.

How he danced, this deaf-boy, danced like a loon to see his tormentor gaping like a fish, the depravity of his intellect silenced forever. How the blood spurted! How it gushed and fountained!

The little clown laughed to see such fun. There was a night's entertainment to be had here, he thought. The axe was his friend forever, keen and wise. It would cut, and cross-cut, it could slice and amputate, yet still they could keep this man alive, if they were cunning enough, alive for a long, long while.

Steve was happy as a lamb. They had the rest of the night ahead of them, and all the music he could possibly want was sounding in his head.

And Quaid knew, meeting the clown's vacant stare through an air turned bloody, that there was worse in the world than dread. Worse than death itself.

There was pain without hope of healing. There was life that refused to end, long after the mind had begged the body to cease. And worst, there were dreams come true.

HELL'S EVENT

Hell came up to the streets and squares of London that September, icy from the depths of the Ninth Circle, too frozen to be warmed even by the swelter of an Indian summer. It had laid its plans as carefully as ever, plans being what they were, and fragile. This time it was perhaps a little more finicky than usual, checking every last detail twice or three times, to be certain it had every chance of winning this vital game.

It had never lacked competitive spirit; it had matched fire against flesh a thousand thousand times down the centuries, sometimes winning, more often losing. Wagers were, after all, the stuff of its advancement. Without the human urge to compete, to bargain, and to bet, Pandemonium might well have fallen for want of citizens. Dancing, dog racing, fiddle-playing: it was all one to the gulfs; all a game in which it might, if it played with sufficient wit, garner a soul or two. That was why Hell came up to London that bright blue day: to run a race, and to win, if it could, enough souls to keep it busy with perdition another age.

Cameron tuned his radio; the voice of the commentator flared and faded as though he was speaking from the

Pole instead of St. Paul's Cathedral. It was still a good half-hour before the race began, but Cameron wanted to listen to the warm-up commentary, just to hear what they were saying about his boy.

". . . atmosphere is electric . . . probably tens of thousands along the route . . ."

The voice disappeared: Cameron cursed, and toyed with the dial until the imbecilities reappeared.

". . . been called the race of the year, and what a day it is! Isn't it, Jim?"

"It certainly is, Mike—"

"That's big Jim Delaney, who's up there in the Eye in the Sky, and he'll be following the race along the route, giving us a bird's eye view, won't you, Jim?"

"I certainly will, Mike—"

"Well, there's a lot of activity behind the line, the competitors are all loosening up for the start. I can see Nick Loyer there, he's wearing number three, and I must say he's looking very fit. He said to me when he arrived he didn't usually like to run on Sundays, but he's made an exception for this race, because of course it's a charity event, and all the proceeds will be going to Cancer Research. Joel Jones, our Gold Medallist in the 800 meters is here, and he'll be running against his great rival Frank McCloud. And besides the big boys we've got a smattering of new faces. Wearing number five, the South African, Malcolm Voight, and completing the field Lester Kinderman, who was of course the surprise winner of the marathon in Austria last year. And I must say they all look fresh as daisies on this superb September afternoon. Couldn't ask for a better day, could we, Jim?"

Joel had woken with bad dreams.

"You'll be fine, stop fretting," Cameron had told him.

But he didn't feel fine; he felt sick in the pit of his stomach. Not pre-race nerves; he was used to those, and he could deal with the feeling. Two fingers down the throat and throw up, that was the best remedy he'd found; get it over and done with. No, this wasn't pre-race nerves, or anything like them. It was deeper, for a start, as though his bowels, to his center, to his source, were cooking.

Cameron had no sympathy.

"It's a charity race, not the Olympics," he said, looking the boy over. "Act your age."

That was Cameron's technique. His mellow voice was made for coaxing, but was used to bully. Without that bullying there would have been no gold medal, no cheering crowds, no admiring girls. One of the tabloids had voted Joel the best loved black face in England. It was good to be greeted as a friend by people he'd never met; he liked the admiration, however short-lived it might turn out to be.

"They love you," said Cameron. "God knows why— they love you."

Then he laughed, his little cruelty over.

"You'll be all right, son," he said. "Get out and run for your life."

Now, in the broad daylight, Joel looked at the rest of the field and felt a little more buoyant. Kinderman had stamina, but he had no finishing power over middle-distance. Marathon technique was a different skill altogether. Besides he was so short-sighted he wore wire-rimmed glasses so thick they gave him the look of a bemused frog. No danger there. Loyer; he was good, but this wasn't really his distance either. He was a hurdler, and a sometime sprinter. 400 meters was his limit and even then he wasn't happy. Voight, the South African. Well, there was not much information on him. Obviously a fit man to judge by the look of him, and someone to watch out for just in case he sprung a surprise. But the real problem of the race was McCloud. Joel had run against Frank "Flash" McCloud three times. Twice beaten him into second place, once (painfully) had the positions reversed. And Frankie boy had a few scores to settle: especially the Olympics defeat; he hadn't liked taking the silver. Frank was the man to watch. Charity race or no charity race McCloud would be running his best, for the crowd and for his pride. He was at the line already testing his starting position, his ears practically pricked. Flash was the man, no doubt of it.

For a moment Joel caught Voight staring at him. Unusual that. Competitors seldom even glanced at each other before a race, it was a kind of coyness. The man's face was pale, and his hair-line was receding. He looked to be in his early thirties, but had a younger, leaner physique. Long legs, big hands. A body somehow out of proportion to his head. When their eyes met, Voight looked away. The fine chain around his neck caught the sun and the crucifix he was wearing glinted gold as it swung gently beneath his chin.

Joel had his good-luck charm with him too. Tucked into the waistband of his shorts, a lock of his mother's hair, which she had plaited for him half a decade ago, before his first major race. She had returned to Barbados the following year, and died there. A great grief: an unforgettable loss. Without Cameron, he would have crumbled.

Cameron watched the preparations from the steps of the Cathedral; he planned to see the start, then ride his bike round the back of the Strand to catch the finish. He'd arrive well before the competitors, and he could keep up with the race on his radio. He felt good with the day. His boy was in fine shape, nausea or no nausea, and the race was an ideal way to keep the lad in a competitive mood without over-stretching him. It was quite a distance of course, across Ludgate Circus, along Fleet Street and past Temple Bar into the Strand, then cutting across the corner of Trafalgar and down Whitehall to the Houses of Parliament. Running on tarmac too. But it was good experience for Joel, and it would pressure him a little, which was useful. There was a distance runner in the boy, and Cameron knew it. He'd never been a sprinter, he couldn't pace himself accurately enough. He needed a distance and time, to find his pulse, to settle down and to work out his tactics. Over 800 meters the boy was a natural: his stride was a model of economy, his rhythm damn-near perfect. But more, he had courage. Courage had won him the gold, and courage would take him first to the finish again and again. That's what made Joel different. Any number of technical whizz-kids came and went, but without courage to supplement those skills they went for almost nothing. To risk when it was worth risking, to run 'til the pain blinded you, that was special and Cameron knew it. He liked to think he'd had a little of himself.

Today, the boy looked less than happy. Women trouble was Cameron's bet. There were always problems with women, especially with the golden boy reputation Joel had garnered. He'd tried to explain that there'd be plenty of time for bed and bawd when his career had run out of steam, but Joel wasn't interested in celibacy, and Cameron didn't altogether blame him.

The pistol was raised, and fired. A plume of blue-white smoke followed by a sound more pop than bang. The shot woke the pigeons from the dome of St. Paul's and they rose in a chattering congregation, their worship interrupted.

Joel was off to a good start. Clean, neat and fast.

The crowd began to call his name immediately, their voices at his back, at his side, a gale of loving enthusiasm.

Cameron watched the first two dozen yards, as the field jockeyed for a running order. Loyer was at the front of the pack, though Cameron wasn't sure whether he'd got there by choice or chance. Joel was behind McCloud, who was behind Loyer. No hurry, boy, said Cameron, and slipped away from the starting line. His bicycle was chained up in Paternoster Row, a minute's walk from the square. He'd always hated cars: godless things, crippling, inhuman, unChristian things. With a bike you were your own master. Wasn't that all a man could ask?

"—And it's a superb start here, to what looks like a potentially marvellous race. They're already across the square and the crowd's going wild here; it really is more like the European Games than a Charity Race. What does it look like to you, Jim?"

"Well Mike, I can see crowds lining the route all the way along Fleet Street: and I've been asked by the police to tell people please not to try and drive down to see the race, because of course all these roads have been cleared for the event, and if you try and drive, really you'll get nowhere."

"Who's got the lead at the moment?"

"Well, Nick Loyer is really setting the pace at this stage in the game, though of course as we know there's going to be a lot of tactical running over this kind of distance. It's more than middle-distance, and it's less than a marathon, but these men are all tacticians, and they'll each be trying to let the other make the running in the early stages."

Cameron always said: let the others be heroes.

That was a hard lesson to learn, Joel had found. When the pistol was fired it was difficult not to go for broke, unwind suddenly like a tight spring. All gone in the first two hundred yards and nothing left in reserve.

It's easy to be a hero, Cameron used to say. It's not clever, it's not clever at all. Don't waste your time showing off, just let the Supermen have their moment. Hang on to the pack, but hold back a little. Better to be cheered at the post because you won than have them call you a good-hearted loser.

Win. Win. Win.

At all costs. At *almost* all costs.

Win.

The man who doesn't want to win is no friend of

mine, he'd say. If you want to do it for the love of it, for the sport of it, do it with somebody else. Only public schoolboys believe that crap about the joy of playing the game. There's no joy for losers, boy. What did I say?

There's no joy for losers.

Be barbaric. Play the rules, but play them to the limit. As far as you can push, push. Let no other sonofabitch tell you differently. You're here to win. What did I say?

Win.

In Paternoster Row the cheering was muted, and the shadows of the buildings blocked the sun. It was almost cold. The pigeons still passed over, unable to settle now they'd been roused from their roost. They were the only occupants of the back streets. The rest of the living world, it seemed, was watching this race.

Cameron unlocked his bicycle, pocketed the chain and padlocks, and hopped on. Pretty healthy for a fifty year old he thought, despite the addiction to cheap cigars. He switched on the radio. Reception was bad, walled in by the buildings; all crackle. He stood astride his bike and tried to improve the tuning. It did a little good.

"—and Nick Loyer is falling behind already—"

That was quick. Mind you, Loyer was past his prime by two or three years. Time to throw in the spike and let the younger men take over. He'd had to do it, though my God it had been painful. Cameron remembered acutely how he'd felt at thirty-three, when he realized that his best running years were over. It was like having one foot buried in the grave, a salutary reminder of how quickly the body blooms and begins to wither.

As he pedalled out of the shadows into a sunnier street a black Mercedes, chauffeur-driven, sailed past, so quietly it could have been wind-propelled. Cameron caught sight of the passengers only briefly. One he recognized as a man Voight had been talking with before the race, a thin faced individual of about forty, with a mouth so tight his lips might have been surgically removed.

Beside him sat Voight.

Impossible as it seemed it was Voight's face that glanced back out of the smoked glass windows; he was even dressed for the race.

Cameron didn't like the look of this at all. He'd seen the South African five minutes earlier, off and running. So who was this? A double obviously. It smelt of a fix, somehow; it stank to high heaven.

The Mercedes was already disappearing around a corner. Cameron turned off the radio and pedalled pell-mell after the car. The balmy sun made him sweat as he rode.

The Mercedes was threading its way through the narrow streets with some difficulty, ignoring all the One Way signs as it went. Its slow passage made it relatively easy for Cameron to keep the vehicle in view without being seen by its occupants, though the effort was beginning to light a fire in his lungs.

In a tiny, nameless alley just west of Fetter Lane, where the shadows were particularly dense, the Mercedes stopped. Cameron, hidden from view round a corner not twenty yards from the car, watched as the door was opened by the chauffeur and the lipless man, with the Voight lookalike close behind, stepped out and went into a nondescript building. When all three had disappeared Cameron propped his bike up against the wall and followed.

The street was pin-drop hushed. From this distance the roar of the crowd was only a murmur. It could have been another world, this street. The flitting shadows of birds, the windows of the buildings bricked up, the peeling paint, the rotten smell in the still air. A dead rabbit lay in the gutter, a black rabbit with a white collar, someone's lost pet. Flies rose and fell on it, alternately startled and ravenous.

Cameron crept towards the open door as quietly as he

was able. He had, as it turned out, nothing to fear. The trio had disappeared down the dark hallway of the house long since. The air was cool in the hall, and smelt of damp. Looking fearless, but feeling afraid, Cameron entered the blind building. The wallpaper in the hallway was shit-colored, the paint the same. It was like walking into a bowel; a dead man's bowel, cold and shitty. Ahead, the stairway had collapsed, preventing access to the upper storey. They had not gone up, but down.

The door to the cellar was adjacent to the defunct staircase, and Cameron could hear voices from below.

No time like the present, he thought, and opened the door sufficiently to squeeze into the dark beyond. It was icy. Not just cold, not damp, but refrigerated. For a moment he thought he'd stepped into a cold storage room. His breath became a mist at his lips: his teeth wanted to chatter.

Can't turn back now, he thought, and started down the frost-slick steps. It wasn't impossibly dark. At the bottom of the flight, a long way down, a pale light flickered, its uninspired glow aspiring to the day. Cameron glanced longingly round at the open door behind him. It looked extremely tempting, but he was curious, so curious. There was nothing to do but descend.

In his nostrils the scent of the place teased. He had a lousy sense of smell, and a worse palate, as his wife was fond of reminding him. She'd say he couldn't distinguish between garlic and a rose, and it was probably true. But the smell in this deep meant something to him, something that stirred the acid in his belly into life.

Goats. It smelt, ha, he wanted to tell her then and there how he'd remembered, it smelt of goats.

He was almost at the bottom of the stairs, twenty, maybe thirty, feet underground. The voices were still some distance away, behind a second door.

He was standing in a little chamber, its walls badly white-washed and scrawled with obscene graffiti, mostly pictures of the sex-act. On the floor, a candelabra, seven forked. Only two of the dingy candles were lit, and they burned with a guttering flame that was almost blue. The goaty smell was stronger now: and mingled with a scent so sickly-sweet it belonged in a Turkish brothel.

Two doors led off the chamber, and from behind one Cameron heard the conversation continuing. With scrupulous caution he crossed the slippery floor to the door, straining to make sense of the murmuring voices. There was an urgency in them.

"—hurry—"

"—the right skills—"

"children, children—"

Laughter.

"I believe we—tomorrow—all of us—"

Laughter again.

Suddenly the voices seemed to change direction, as if the speakers were moving back towards the door. Cameron took three steps back across the icy floor, almost colliding with the candelabra. The flames spat and whispered in the chamber as he passed.

He had to choose either the stairs or the other door. The stairs represented utter retreat. If he climbed them he'd be safe, but he would never know. Never know why the cold, why the blue flames, why the smell of goats. The door was a chance. Back to it, his eyes on the door opposite, he fought with the bitingly cold brass handle. It turned with some tussling, and he ducked out of sight as the door opposite opened. The two movements were perfectly syncopated: God was with him.

Even as he closed the door he knew he'd made an error. God wasn't with him at all.

Needles of cold penetrated his head, his teeth, his eyes, his fingers. He felt as though he'd been thrown naked into the heart of an iceberg. His blood seemed to stand still in his veins: the spit of his tongue crystallized: the mucus on the lining of his nose pricked as it turned to ice. The cold seemed to cripple him: he couldn't even turn round.

Barely able to move his joints, he fumbled for his cig-arette lighter with fingers so numb they could have been cut off without him feeling it.

The lighter was already glued to his hand, the sweat on his fingers had turned to frost. He tried to ignite it, against the dark, against the cold. Reluctantly it sparked into a spluttering half-life.

The room was large: an ice-cavern. Its walls, its en-crusted roof, sparkled and shone. Stalactites of ice, lance-sharp, hung over his head. The floor on which he stood, poised uncertainly, was raked towards a hole in the middle of the room. Five or six feet across, its edges and walls were so lined with ice it seemed as though a river had been arrested as it poured down into the darkness.

He thought of *Xanadu,* a poem he knew by heart. Vi-sions of another Albion—

> "Where Alph the sacred river ran,
> Through caverns measureless to man,
> Down to a sunless sea."

If there was indeed a sea down there, it was a frozen sea. It was death forever.

It was as much as he could do to keep upright, to pre-vent himself from sliding down the incline towards the unknown. The lighter flickered as an icy air blew it out.

"Shit," said Cameron as he was plunged into dark-ness.

Whether the word alerted the trio outside, or whether God deserted him totally at that moment and invited them to open the door, he would never know. But as the door swung wide it pushed Cameron off his feet. Too numb and too frozen to prevent his fall he collapsed to the ice floor as the smell of the goat wafted into the room.

Cameron half turned. Voight's double was at the door, as was the chauffeur, and the third man in the Mercedes. He wore a coat apparently made of several goat-skins. The hooves and the horns still hung from it. The blood on its fur was brown and gummy.

"What are you doing here, Mr. Cameron?" asked the goat-coated man.

Cameron could barely speak. The only feeling left in his head was a pin-point of agony in the middle of his forehead.

"What the hell is going on?" he said, through lips almost too frozen to move.

"Precisely that, Mr. Cameron," the man replied. "Hell is going on."

As they ran past St. Mary-le-Strand, Loyer glanced behind him, and stumbled. Joel, a full three meters behind the leaders, knew the man was giving up. So quickly too; there was something amiss. He slackened his pace, letting McCloud and Voight pass him. No great hurry. Kinderman was quite a way behind, unable to compete with these fast boys. He was the tortoise in this race, for sure. Loyer was overtaken by McCloud, then Voight, and finally Jones and Kinderman. His breath had suddenly deserted him, and his legs felt like lead. Worse, he was seeing the tarmac under his running shoes creaking and cracking, and fingers, like loveless children, seeking up out of the ground to touch him. Nobody else was seeing them, it seemed. The crowds just roared on, while these illusory hands broke out of their tarmac graves and secured a hold on him. He collapsed into their dead arms exhausted, his youth broken and his strength spent. The enquiring fingers of the dead continued to pluck at him, long after the doctors had removed him from the track, examined him and sedated him.

He knew why, of course, lying there on the hot tarmac while they had their pricking way with him. He'd looked behind him. That's what made them come. He'd looked—

"And after Loyer's sensational collapse, the race is

open wide. Frank the Flash McCloud is setting the pace now, and he's really speeding away from the new boy, Voight. Joel Jones is even further behind, he doesn't seem to be keeping up with the leaders at all. What do you think, Jim?''

''Well he's either pooped already, or he's really taking a chance that they'll exhaust themselves. Remember he's new over this distance—''

''Yes, Jim—''

''And that might make him careless. Certainly he's going to have to do a lot of work to improve on his present position in third place.''

Joel felt giddy. For a moment, as he'd watched Loyer begin to lose his grip on the race, he'd heard the man praying out loud. Praying to God to save him. He'd been the only one who heard the words—

> ''Yea, though I walk through the
> shadows of the Valley of Death I shall
> fear no evil, for thou art with
> me, thy rod and thy staff they—''

The sun was hotter now, and Joel was beginning to feel the familiar voices of his tiring limbs. Running on tarmac was hard on the feet, hard on the joints. Not that that would make a man take to praying. He tried to put Loyer's desperation out of his mind, and concentrate on the matter in hand.

There was still a lot of running to do, the race was not even half over. Plenty of time to catch up with the heroes: plenty of time.

As he ran, his brain idly turned over the prayers his mother had taught him in case he should need one, but the years had eroded them: they were all but gone.

''My name,'' said the goat-coated man, ''is Gregory Burgess. Member of Parliament. You wouldn't know me. I try to keep a low profile.''

"MP?" said Cameron.

"Yes. Independent. *Very* independent."

"Is that Voight's brother?"

Burgess glanced at Voight's other self. He was not even shivering in the intense cold, despite the fact that he was only wearing a thin singlet and shorts.

"Brother?" Burgess said. "No, no. He is my—what is the word? Familiar."

The word rang a bell, but Cameron wasn't well-read. What was a familiar?

"Show him," said Burgess magnanimously.

Voight's face shook, the skin seeming to shrivel, the lips curling back from the teeth, the teeth melting into a white wax that poured down a gullet that was itself transfiguring into a column of shimmering silver. The face was no longer human, no longer even mammalian. It had become a fan of knives, their blades glistening in the candlelight through the door. Even as this bizarrerie became fixed, it started to change again, the knives melting and darkening, fur sprouting, eyes appearing and swelling to balloon size. Antennae leapt from this new head, mandibles were extruded from the pulp of transfiguration, and the head of a bee, huge and perfectly intricate, now sat on Voight's neck.

Burgess obviously enjoyed the display; he applauded with gloved hands.

"Familiars both," he said, gesturing to the chauffeur, who had removed the cap, and let a welter of auburn hair fall to her shoulders. She was ravishingly beautiful, a face to give your life for. But an illusion, like the other. No doubt capable of infinite personae.

"They're both mine, of course," said Burgess proudly.

"What?" was all Cameron could manage; he hoped it stood for all the questions in his head.

"I serve Hell, Mr. Cameron. And in its turn Hell serves me."

"Hell?"

"Behind you, one of the entrances to the Ninth Circle. You know your Dante, I presume?

"Lo! Dis; and lo! the place
Where thou has need to arm thy heart with strength."

"Why are you here?"

"To run this race. Or rather my third familiar is already running the race. He will not be beaten this time. This time it is Hell's event, Mr. Cameron, and we shall not be cheated of the prize."

"Hell," said Cameron.

"You believe, don't you? You're a good church-goer. Still pray before you eat, like any God-fearing soul. Afraid of choking on your dinner."

"How do you know I pray?"

"Your wife told me. Oh, your wife was very informative about you, Mr. Cameron, she really opened up to me. Very accommodating. A confirmed analyst, after my attentions. She gave me so much . . . information. You're a good Socialist, aren't you, like your father."

"Politics now—"

"Oh, politics is the hub of the issue, Mr. Cameron. Without politics we're lost in a wilderness, aren't we? Even Hell needs order. Nine great circles: a pecking order of punishments. Look down; see for yourself."

Cameron could feel the hole at his back: he didn't need to look.

"We stand for order, you know. Not chaos. That's just heavenly propaganda. And you know what we'll win?"

"It's a charity race."

"Charity is the least of it. We're not running this race to save the world from cancer. We're running it for government."

Cameron half-grasped the point.

"Government," he said.

"Once every century this race is run from St. Paul's

to the Palace of Westminster. Often it has been run at the dead of night, unheralded, unapplauded. Today it is run in full sunshine, watched by thousands. But whatever the circumstance, it is always the same race. Your athletes, against one of ours. If you win, another hundred years of democracy. If we win . . . as we will . . . the end of the world as you know it.''

At his back Cameron felt a vibration. The expression on Burgess' face had abruptly changed; the confidence had become clouded, the smugness was instantly replaced by a look of nervous excitement.

''Well, well,'' he said, his hands flapping like birds. ''It seems we are about to be visited by higher powers. How flattering—''

Cameron turned, and peered over the edge of the hole. It didn't matter how curious he was now. They had him; he may as well see all there was to see.

A wave of icy air blew up from the sunless circle and in the darkness of the shaft he could see a shape approaching. Its movement was steady, and its face was thrown back to look at the world.

Cameron could hear its breathing, see the wound of its features open and close in the murk, oily bone locking and unlocking like the face of a crab.

Burgess was on his knees, the two familiars flat on the floor to either side of him, faces to the ground.

Cameron knew he would have no other chance. He stood up, his limbs hardly in his control, and blundered towards Burgess, whose eyes were closed in reverent prayer. More by accident than intention his knee caught Burgess under the jaw as he passed, and the man was sent sprawling. Cameron's soles slid on the floor out of the ice-cavern and into the candlelit chamber beyond.

Behind him, the room was filling with smoke and sighs, and Cameron, like Lot's wife fleeing from the destruction of Sodom, glanced back just once to see the forbidden sight behind him.

It was emerging from the shaft, its grey bulk filling

the hole, lit by some radiance from below. Its eyes, deep-set in the naked bone of its elephantine head, met Cameron's through the open door. They seemed to touch him like a kiss, entering his thoughts through his eyes.

He was not turned to salt. Pulling his curious glance away from the face, he skated across the ante-chamber and started to climb the stairs two and three at a time, falling and climbing, falling and climbing. The door was still ajar. Beyond it, daylight and the world.

He flung the door open and collapsed into the hall-way, feeling the warmth already beginning to wake his frozen nerves. There was no noise on the stairs behind him: clearly they were too in awe of their fleshless visitor to follow him. He hauled himself along the wall of the hallway, his body wracked with shivers and chatter-ings.

Still they didn't follow.

Outside the day was blindingly bright, and he began to feel the exhilaration of escape. It was like nothing he'd ever felt before. To have been so close, yet survived. God had been with him after all.

He staggered along the road back to his bicycle, determined to stop the race, to tell the world—

His bike was untouched, its handlebars warm as his wife's arms.

As he hooked his leg over, the look he had exchanged with Hell caught fire. His body, ignorant of the heat in his brain, continued about its business for a moment, putting its feet on the pedals and starting to ride away.

Cameron felt the ignition in his head and knew he was dead.

The look, the glance behind him—

Lot's wife.

Like Lot's stupid wife—

The lightning leapt between his ears: faster than thought.

His skull cracked, and the lightning, white-hot, shot

out from the furnace of his brain. His eyes withered to black nuts in his sockets, he belched light from mouth and nostrils. The combustion turned him into a column of black flesh in a matter of seconds, without a flame or a wisp of smoke.

Cameron's body was completely incinerated by the time the bicycle careered off the road and crashed through the tailor's shop window, where it lay like a dummy, face down amongst the ashen suits. He, too, had looked back.

The crowds at Trafalgar Square were a seething mass of enthusiasm. Cheers, tears and flags. It was as though this little race had become something special for these people: a ritual the significance of which they could not know. Yet somewhere in them they understood the day was laden with sulphur, they sensed their lives stood on tiptoe to reach heaven. Especially the children. They ran along the route, shouting incoherent blessings, their faces squeezed up with their fears. Some called his name.

"Joel! Joel!"

Or did he imagine that? Had he imagined, too, the prayer from Loyer's lips, and the signs in the radiant faces of the babies held high to watch the runners pass?

As they turned into Whitehall Frank McCloud glanced confidentially over his shoulder and Hell took him.

It was sudden: it was simple.

He stumbled, an icy hand in his chest crushing the life out of him. Joel slowed as he approached the man. His face was purple: his lips foamy.

"McCloud," he said, and stopped to stare in his great rival's thin face.

McCloud looked up at him from behind a veil of smoke that had turned his grey eyes ocher. Joel reached down to help him.

"Don't touch me," McCloud growled. The filament

vessels in his eyes bulged and bled.

"Cramp?" asked Joel. "Is it cramp?"

"Run you bastard, run," McCloud was saying at him, as the hand in his innards seized his life out. He was oozing blood through the pores on his face now, weeping red tears. "Run. And don't look back. For Christ's sake, *don't look back*."

"What is it?"

"Run for your life!"

The words weren't requests but imperatives.

Run.

Not for gold or glory. Just to live.

Joel glanced up, suddenly aware that there was some huge-headed thing at his back, cold breath on his neck.

He picked up his heels and *ran*.

"—Well, things aren't going so well for the runners here, Jim. After Loyer going down so sensationally, now Frank McCloud has stumbled too. I've never seen anything quite like it. But he seems to have had a few words with Joel Jones as he ran past, so he must be OK."

McCloud was dead by the time they put him in the ambulance, and putrefied by the following morning.

Joel ran. Jesus, did he run. The sun had become ferocious in his face, washing the color out of the cheering crowds, out of the faces, out of the flags. Everything was one sheet of noise, drained of humanity.

Joel knew the feeling that was coming over him, the sense of dislocation that accompanied fatigue and over-oxygenation. He was running in a bubble of his own consciousness, thinking, sweating, suffering by himself, for himself, in the name of himself.

And it wasn't so bad, this being alone. Songs began to fill his head: snatches of hymns, sweet phrases from love-songs, dirty rhymes. His self idled, and his dream-mind, unnamed and fearless, took over.

Ahead, washed by the same white rain of light, was Voight. That was the enemy, that was the thing to be surpassed. Voight, with his shining crucifix rocking in the sun. He could do it, as long as he didn't look, as long as he didn't look—

Behind him.

Burgess opened the door of the Mercedes and climbed in. Time had been wasted: valuable time. He should be at the Houses of Parliament, at the finishing line, ready to welcome the runners home. There was a scene to play, in which he would pretend the mild and smiling face of democracy. And tomorrow? Not so mild.

His hands were clammy with excitement, and his pinstripe suit smelt of the goat-skin coat he was obliged to wear in the room. Still, nobody would notice; and even if they did what Englishman would be so impolite to mention that he smelt goaty?

He hated the Lower Chamber, the perpetual ice, that damn yawning hole with its distant sound of loss. But all that was over now. He'd made his oblations, he'd shown his utter and ceaseless adoration of the pit; now it was time to reap the rewards.

As they drove, he thought of his many sacrifices to ambition. At first, minor stuff: kittens and cockerels. Later, he was to discover how ridiculous they thought such gestures were. But at the beginning he'd been innocent: not knowing what to give or how to give it. They began to make their requirements clear as the years went by, and he, in time, learnt to practice the etiquette of selling his soul. His self mortifications were studiously planned and immaculately staged, though they had left him without nipples or the hope of children. It was worth the pain, though: the power came to him by degrees. A triple first at Oxford, a wife endowed beyond the dreams of priapism, a seat in Parliament, and soon, soon enough, the country itself.

The cauterized stumps of his thumbs ached, as they often did when he was nervous. Idly, he sucked on one.

•　•　•

"—Well we're now in the closing stages of what really has been one hell of a race, eh, Jim?"

"Oh yes, it's really been a revelation, hasn't it? Voight is really the outsider of the field; and here he is streaking away from the competition without much effort. Of course, Jones made the unselfish gesture of checking with Frank McCloud that he was indeed all right after that bad fall of his, and that put him behind."

"It's lost the race for Jones really, hasn't it?"

"I think that's right. I think it's lost the race for him."

"This is a charity race, of course."

"Absolutely. And in a situation like this it's not whether you win or lose—"

"It's how you play the game."

"Right."

"Right."

"Well they're both in sight of the Houses of Parliament now as they come round the bend of Whitehall. And the crowds are cheering their boy on, but I really think it's a lost cause—"

"Mind you, he brought something special out of the bag in Sweden."

"He did. He did."

"Maybe he'll do it again."

Joel ran, and the gap between himself and Voight was beginning to close. He concentrated on the man's back, his eyes boring into his shirt, learning his rhythm, looking for weaknesses.

There was a slowing there. The man was not as fast as he had been. An unevenness had crept into his stride, a sure sign of fatigue.

He could take him. With courage, he could take him . . .

And Kinderman. He'd forgotten about Kinderman. Without thinking, Joel glanced over his shoulder and looked behind him.

Kinderman was way back, still keeping his steady, marathon runner's pace unchanged. But there was something else behind Joel: another runner, almost on his heels; ghostly, vast.

He averted his eyes and stared ahead, cursing his stupidity.

He was gaining on Voight with every pace. The man was really running out of steam, quite clearly. Joel knew he could take him for certain, if he worked at it. Forget his pursuer, whatever if was, forget everything except overtaking Voight.

But the sight at his back wouldn't leave his head.

"Don't look back": McCloud's words. Too late, he'd done it. Better to know then who this phantom was.

He looked again.

At first he saw nothing, just Kinderman jogging along. And then the ghost runner appeared once more and he knew what had brought McCloud and Loyer down.

It was no runner, living or dead. It wasn't even human. A smoky body, and yawning darkness for its head, it was Hell itself that was pressing on him.

"Don't look back."

Its mouth, if mouth it was, was open. Breath so cold it made Joel gasp swirled around him. That was why Loyer had muttered prayers as he ran. Much good it had done him; death had come anyway.

Joel looked away, not caring to see Hell so close, trying to ignore the sudden weakness in his knees.

Now Voight, too, was glancing behind him. The look on his face was dark and uneasy: and Joel knew somehow that he belonged to Hell, that the shadow behind him was Voight's master.

"Voight, Voight. Voight. Voight—" Joel expelled the word with every stride.

Voight heard his name being spoken.

"Black bastard," he said aloud.

Joel's stride lengthened a little. He was within two meters of Hell's runner.

"Look . . . Behind . . . You," said Voight.

"I see it."

"It's . . . come . . . for . . . you."

The words were mere melodrama: two-dimensional. *He* was master of his body, wasn't he? And he was not afraid of darkness, he was painted in it. Wasn't that what made him less than human as far as so many people were concerned? Or more, more than human; bloodier, sweatier, fleshier. More arm, more leg, more head. More strength, more appetite. What could Hell do? Eat him? He'd taste foul on the palate. Freeze him? He was too hot-blooded, too fast, too living.

Nothing would take him, he was a barbarian with the manners of a gentleman.

Neither night nor day entirely.

Voight was suffering: his pain was in his torn breath, in the gangling rags of his stride. They were just fifty meters from the steps and the finishing line, but Voight's lead was being steadily eroded; each step brought the runners closer.

Then the bargains began.

"Listen . . . to . . . me."

"What are you?"

"Power . . . I'll get you power . . . just . . . let . . . us . . . win."

Joel was almost at his side now.

"Too late."

His legs elated: his mind span with pleasure. Hell behind him: Hell beside him, what did he care? He could run.

He passed Voight, joints fluent: an easy machine.

"Bastard. Bastard. Bastard—" the familiar was saying, his face contorted with the agonies of stress. And didn't that face flicker as Joel passed it by? Didn't its features seem to lose, momentarily, the illusion of being human?

Then Voight was falling behind him, and the crowds were cheering, and the colors were flooding back into the world. It was victory ahead. He didn't know for what cause, but victory nevertheless.

There was Cameron, he saw him now, standing on the steps beside a man Joel didn't know, a man in a pin-stripe suit. Cameron was smiling and shouting with uncharacteristic enthusiasm, beckoning to Joel from the steps.

He ran, if anything, a little faster towards the finishing line, his strength coaxed by Cameron's face.

Then the face seemed to change. Was it the heat haze that made his hair shimmer? No, the flesh of his cheeks was bubbling now, and there were dark patches growing darker still on his neck, at his forehead. Now his hair was rising from his head and cremating light was flickering up from his scalp. Cameron was burning. Cameron was burning, and still the smile, and still the beckoning hand.

Joel felt sudden despair.

Hell behind. Hell in front.

This wasn't Cameron. Cameron was nowhere to be seen: so Cameron was gone.

He knew it in his gut. Cameron was gone: and this black parody that smiled at him and welcomed him was his last moments, replayed for the delight of his admirers.

Joel's step faltered, the rhythm of his stride lost. At his back he heard Voight's breath, horridly thick, close, closer.

His whole body suddenly revolted. His stomach demanded to throw up its contents, his legs cried out to collapse, his head refused to think, only to fear.

"Run," he said to himself. "Run. Run. Run."

But Hell was ahead. How could he run into the arms of such foulness?

Voight had closed the gap between them, and was at his shoulder, jostling him as he passed. The victory was being snatched from Joel easily: sweets from a babe.

The finishing line was a dozen strides away, and Voight had the lead again. Scarcely aware of what he was doing, Joel reached out and snatched at Voight as he ran, grabbing his singlet. It was a cheat, clear to everybody in the crowd. But what the Hell.

He pulled hard at Voight, and both men stumbled. The crowd parted as they veered off the track and fell heavily, Voight on top of Joel.

Joel's arm, flung out to prevent him falling too heavily, was crushed under the weight of both bodies. Caught badly, the bone of his forearm cracked. Joel heard it snap a moment before he felt the spasm; then the pain threw a cry out of his mouth.

On the steps, Burgess was screeching like a wild man. Quite a performance. Cameras were snapping, commentators commenting.

"Get up! Get up!" the man was yelling.

But Joel had snatched Voight with his one good arm, and nothing was going to make him let go.

The two rolled around in the gravel, every roll crushing Joel's arm and sending spurts of nausea through his gut.

The familiar playing Voight was exhausted. It had never been so tired: unprepared for the stress of the race its master had demanded it run. Its temper was short, its control perilously close to snapping. Joel could smell its breath on his face, and it was the smell of a goat.

"Show yourself," he said.

The thing's eyes had lost their pupils: they were all white now. Joel hawked up a clot of phlegm from the back of his thick-spittled mouth and spat it in the familiar's face.

Its temper broke.

The face dissolved. What had seemed to be flesh sprouted into a new resemblance, a devouring trap without eyes or nose, or ears, or hair.

All around, the crowd shrank back. People shrieked: people fainted. Joel saw none of this: but heard the cries with satisfaction. This transformation was not just for his benefit: it was common knowledge. They were seeing it all, the truth, the filthy, gaping truth.

The mouth was huge, and lined with teeth like the maw of some deep-water fish, ridiculously large. Joel's one good arm was under its lower jaw, just managing to keep it at bay, as he cried for help.

Nobody stepped forward.

The crowd stood at a polite distance, still screaming, still staring, unwilling to interfere. It was purely a spectator sport, wrestling with the Devil. Nothing to do with them.

Joel felt the last of his strength falter: his arm could keep the mouth at bay no longer. Despairing, he felt the teeth at his brow and at his chin, felt them pierce his flesh and his bone, felt, finally, the white night invade him, as the mouth bit off his face.

The familiar rose up from the corpse with strands of Joel's head hanging out from between its teeth. It had taken off the features like a mask, leaving a mess of blood and jerking muscle. In the open hole of Joel's mouth the root of his tongue flapped and spurted, past speaking sorrow.

Burgess didn't care how he appeared to the world. The race was everything: a victory was a victory however it was won. And Jones had cheated after all.

"Here!" he yelled to the familiar. "Heel!"

It turned its blood-strung face to him.

"Come here," Burgess ordered it.

They were only a few yards apart: a few strides to the line and the race was won.

"Run to me!" Burgess screeched. "Run! Run! Run!"

The familiar was weary, but it knew its master's voice. It loped towards the line, blindly following Burgess' calls.

Four paces. Three—

And Kinderman ran past it to the line. Short-sighted Kinderman, a pace ahead of Voight, took the race without knowing the victory he had won, without even seeing the horrors that were sprawled at his feet.

There were no cheers as he passed the line. No congratulations.

The air around the steps seemed to darken, and an unseasonal frost appeared in the air.

Shaking his head apologetically, Burgess fell to his knees.

"Our Father, who wert in Heaven, unhallowed be thy name—"

Such an old trick. Such a naïve response.

The crowd began to back away. Some people were already running. Children, knowing the nature of the dark having been so recently touched by it, were the least troubled. They took their parents' hands and led them away from the spot like lambs, telling them not to look behind them, and their parents half-remembered the womb, the first tunnel, the first aching exit from a hallowed place, the first terrible temptation to look behind and die. Remembering, they went with their children.

Only Kinderman seemed untouched. He sat on the steps and cleaned his glasses, smiling to have won, indifferent to the chill.

Burgess, knowing his prayers were insufficient, turned tail and disappeared into the Palace of Westminster.

The familiar, deserted, relinquished all claim to human appearance and became itself. Insolid, insipid, it spat out the foul-tasting flesh of Joel Jones. Half chewed, the runner's face lay on the gravel beside his body. The familiar folded itself into the air and went back to the Circle it called home.

It was stale in the corridors of power: no life, no help.

Burgess was out of condition, and his running soon became a walk. A steady step along the gloom-panelled corridors, his feet almost silent on the well trodden carpet.

He didn't quite know what to do. Clearly he would be

blamed for his failure to plan against all eventualities, but he was confident he could argue his way out of that. He would give them whatever they required as recompense for his lack of foresight. An ear, a foot; he had nothing to lose but flesh and blood.

But he had to plan his defense carefully, because they hated bad logic. It was more than his life was worth to come before them with half-formed excuses.

There was a chill behind him; he knew what it was. Hell had followed him along these silent corridors, even into the very womb of democracy. He would survive though, as long as he didn't turn round: as long as he kept his eyes on the floor, or on his thumbless hands, no harm would come to him. That was one of the first lessons one learnt, dealing with the gulfs.

There was a frost in the air. Burgess' breath was visible in front of him, and his head was aching with cold.

"I'm sorry," he said sincerely to his pursuer.

The voice that came back to him was milder than he'd expected.

"It wasn't your fault."

"No," said Burgess, taking confidence from its conciliatory tone. "It was an error and I am contrite. I overlooked Kinderman."

"That was a mistake. We all make them," said Hell. "Still, in another hundred years, we'll try again. Democracy is still a new cult: it's not lost its superficial glamour yet. We'll give it another century, and have the best of them then."

"Yes."

"But you—"

"I know."

"No power for you, Gregory."

"No."

"It's not the end of the world. Look at me."

"Not at the moment, if you don't mind."

Burgess kept walking, steady step upon steady step. Keep it calm, keep it rational.

"Look at me, please, " Hell cooed.

"Later, sir."

"I'm only asking you to look at me. A little respect would be appreciated."

"I will. I will, really. Later."

The corridor divided here. Burgess took the left-hand fork. He thought the symbolism might flatter. It was a cul-de-sac.

Burgess stood still facing the wall. The cold air was in his marrow, and the stumps of his thumbs were really giving him jip. He took off his gloves and sucked, hard.

"Look at me. Turn and look at me," said the courteous voice.

What was he to do now? Back out of the corridor and find another way was best, presumably. He'd just have to walk around and around in circles until he'd argued his point sufficiently well for his pursuer to leave him be.

As he stood, juggling the alternatives available to him, he felt a slight ache in his neck.

"Look at me," the voice said again.

And his throat was constricted. There was, strangely, a grinding in his head, the sound of bone rasping bone. It felt like a knife was lodged in the base of his skull.

"Look at me," Hell said one final time, and Burgess' head turned.

Not his body. That stayed standing facing the blank wall of the cul-de-sac.

But his head cranked around on its slender axis, disregarding reason and anatomy. Burgess choked as his gullet twisted on itself like a flesh rope, his vertebrae screwed to powder, his cartilage to fiber mush. His eyes bled, his ears popped, and he died, looking at that sunless, unbegotten face.

"I told you to look at me," said Hell, and went its bitter way, leaving him standing there, a fine paradox for the democrats to find when they came, bustling with words, into the Palace of Westminster.

JACQUELINE ESS:
HER WILL AND TESTAMENT

My God, she thought, this can't be living. Day in, day out: the boredom, the drudgery, the frustration.

My Christ, she prayed, let me out, set me free, crucify me if you must, but put me out of my misery.

In lieu of his euthanasian benediction, she took a blade from Ben's razor, one dull day in late March, locked herself in the bathroom, and slit her wrists.

Through the throbbing in her ears, she faintly heard Ben outside the bathroom door.

"Are you in there, darling?"

"Go away," she thought she said.

"I'm back early, sweetheart. The traffic was light."

"Please go away."

The effort of trying to speak slid her off the toilet seat and on to the white-tiled floor, where pools of her blood were already cooling.

"Darling?"

"Go."

"Darling."

"Away."

"Are you all right?"

Now he was rattling at the door, the rat. Didn't he realize she couldn't open it, wouldn't open it?

"Answer me, Jackie."

She groaned. She couldn't stop herself. The pain wasn't as terrible as she'd expected, but there was an ugly feeling, as though she'd been kicked in the head. Still, he couldn't catch her in time, not now. Not even if he broke the door down.

He broke the door down.

She looked up at him through an air grown so thick with death you could have sliced it.

"Too late," she thought she said.

But it wasn't.

My God, she thought, this can't be suicide. I haven't died.

The doctor Ben had hired for her was too perfectly benign. Only the best, he'd promised, only the very best for my Jackie.

"It's nothing," the doctor reassured her, "that we can't put right with a little tinkering."

Why doesn't he just come out with it? she thought. He doesn't give a damn. He doesn't know what it's like.

"I deal with a lot of these women's problems," he confided, fairly oozing a practiced compassion. "It's got to epidemic proportions among a certain age-bracket."

She was barely thirty. What was he telling her? That she was prematurely menopausal?

"Depression, partial or total withdrawal, neuroses of every shape and size. You're not alone, believe me."

Oh yes I am, she thought. I'm here in my head, on my own, and you can't know what it's like.

"We'll have you right in two shakes of a lamb's tail."

I'm a lamb, am I? Does he think I'm a lamb?

Musing, he glanced up at his framed qualifications, then at his manicured nails, then at the pens on his desk and notepad. But he didn't look at Jacqueline. Anywhere but at Jacqueline.

"I know," he was saying now, "what you've been

through, and it's been traumatic. Women have certain needs. If they go unanswered—''

What would he know about women's needs?

You're not a woman, she thought she thought.

"What?" he said.

Had she spoken? She shook her head: denying speech. He went on; finding his rhythm once more: "I'm not going to put you through interminable therapy-sessions. You don't want that, do you? You want a little reassurance, and you want something to help you sleep at nights."

He was irritating her badly now. His condescension was so profound it had no bottom. All-knowing, all-seeing Father; that was his performance. As if he were blessed with some miraculous insight into the nature of a woman's soul.

"Of course, I've tried therapy courses with patients in the past. But between you and me—"

He lightly patted her hand. Father's palm on the back of her hand. She was supposed to be flattered, reassured, maybe even seduced.

"—between you and me it's so much talk. Endless talk. Frankly, what good does it do? We've all got problems. You can't talk them away, can you?"

You're not a woman. You don't look like a woman, you don't feel like a woman—

"Did you say something?"

She shook her head.

"I thought you said something. Please feel free to be honest with me."

She didn't reply, and he seemed to tire of pretending intimacy. He stood up and went to the window.

"I think the best thing for you—"

He stood against the light: darkening the room, obscuring the view of the cherry trees on the lawn through the window. She stared at his wide shoulders, at his narrow hips. A fine figure of a man, as Ben would have called him. No child-bearer he. Made to remake the world, a body like that. If not the world, remaking minds would have to do.

"I think the best thing for you—"

What did he know, with his hips, with his shoulders? He was too much a man to understand anything of her.

"I think the best thing for you would be a course of sedatives—"

Now her eyes were on his waist.

"—and a holiday."

Her mind had focussed now on the body beneath the veneer of his clothes. The muscle, bone and blood beneath the elastic skin. She pictured it from all sides, sizing it up, judging its powers of resistance, then closing on it. She thought:

Be a woman.

Simply, as she thought that preposterous idea, it began to take shape. Not a fairy-tale transformation, unfortunately, his flesh resisted such magic. She willed his manly chest into making breasts of itself and it began to swell most fetchingly, until the skin burst and his sternum flew apart. His pelvis, teased to breaking point, fractured at its center; unbalanced, he toppled over on to his desk and from there stared up at her, his face yellow with shock. He licked his lips, over and over again, to find some wetness to talk with. His mouth was dry: his words were still-born. It was from between his legs that all the noise was coming; the splashing of his blood; the thud of his bowel on the carpet.

She screamed at the absurd monstrosity she had made, and withdrew to the far corner of the room, where she was sick in the pot of the rubber plant.

My God, she thought, this can't be murder. I didn't so much as touch him.

What Jacqueline had done that afternoon, she kept to herself. No sense in giving people sleepless nights, thinking about such peculiar talent.

The police were very kind. They produced any number of explanations for the sudden departure of Dr. Blandish, though none quite described how his chest had erupted in that extraordinary fashion, making two handsome (if hairy) domes of his pectorals.

It was assumed that some unknown psychotic, strong in his insanity, had broken in, done the deed with hands, hammers and saws, and exited, locking the innocent Jacqueline Ess in an appalled silence no interrogation could hope to penetrate.

Person or persons unknown had clearly dispatched the doctor to where neither sedatives nor therapy could help him.

She almost forgot for a while. But as the months passed it came back to her by degrees, like a memory of a secret adultery. It teased her with its forbidden delights. She forgot the nausea, and remembered the power. She forgot sordidity, and remembered strength. She forgot the guilt that had seized her afterwards and longed, longed to do it again.

Only better.

"Jacqueline."

Is this my husband, she thought, actually calling me by my name? Usually it was Jackie, or Jack, or nothing at all.

"Jacqueline."

He was looking at her with those big baby blues of his, like the college-boy she'd loved at first sight. But his mouth was harder now, and his kisses tasted like stale bread.

"Jacqueline."

"Yes."

"I've got something I want to speak to you about."

A conversation? she thought, it must be a public holiday.

"I don't know how to tell you this."

"Try me," she suggested.

She knew that she could think his tongue into speaking if it pleased her. Make him tell her what she wanted to hear. Words of love, maybe, if she could remember what they sounded like. But what was the use of that? Better the truth.

"Darling, I've gone off the rails a bit."

"What do you mean?" she said.

Have you, you bastard, she thought.

"It was while you weren't quite yourself. You know, when things had more or less stopped between us. Separate rooms . . . you wanted separate rooms . . . and I just went bananas with fustration. I didn't want to upset you, so I didn't say anything. But it's no use me trying to live two lives."

"You can have an affair if you want to, Ben."

"It's not an affair, Jackie. I love her—"

He was preparing one of his speeches, she could see it gathering momentum behind his teeth. The justifications that became accusations, those excuses that always turned into assaults on her character. Once he got into full flow there'd be no stopping him. She didn't want to hear.

"—she's not like you at all, Jackie. She's frivolous in her way. I suppose you'd call her shallow."

It might be worth interrupting here, she thought, before he ties himself in his usual knots.

"She's not moody like you. You know, she's just a normal woman. I don't mean to say you're not normal: you can't help having depressions. But she's not so sensitive."

"There's no need, Ben—"

"No, damn it, I want it all off my chest."

On to me, she thought.

"You've never let me explain," he was saying. "You've always given me one of those damn looks of yours, as if you wished I'd—"

Die.

"—wished I'd shut up."

Shut up.

"You don't care how I feel!" He was shouting now. "Always in your own little world."

Shut up, she thought.

His mouth was open. She seemed to wish it closed, and with the thought his jaws snapped together, severing the very tip of his pink tongue. It fell from between his lips and lodged in a fold of his shirt.

Shut up, she thought again.

The two perfect regiments of his teeth ground down into each other, cracking and splitting, nerve, calcium and spit making a pinkish foam on his chin as his mouth collapsed inwards.

Shut up, she was still thinking as his startled baby blues sank back into his skull and his nose wormed its way into his brain.

He was not Ben any longer, he was a man with a red lizard's head, flattening, battening down upon itself, and, thank God, he was past speech-making once and for all.

Now she had the knack of it, she began to take pleasure in the changes she was willing upon him.

She flipped him head over heels on to the floor and began to compress his arms and legs, telescoping flesh and resistant bone into a smaller and yet smaller space. His clothes were folded inwards, and the tissue of his stomach was plucked from his neatly packaged entrails and stretched around his body to wrap him up. His fingers were poking from his shoulder-blades now, and his feet, still thrashing with fury, were tipped up in his gut. She turned him over one final time to pressure his spine into a foot-long column of muck, and that was about the end of it.

As she came out of her ecstasy she saw Ben sitting on the floor, shut up into a space about the size of one of his fine leather suitcases, while blood, bile and lymphatic fluid pulsed weakly from his hushed body.

My God, she thought, this can't be my husband. He's never been as tidy as that.

This time she didn't wait for help. This time she knew

what she'd done (guessed, even, how she'd done it) and she accepted her crime for the too-rough justice it was. She packed her bags and left the home.

I'm alive, she thought. For the first time in my whole, wretched life, I'm alive.

Vassi's Testimony (part one)

"To you who dream of sweet, strong women I leave this story. It is a promise, as surely as it is a confession, as surely as it's the last words of a lost man who wanted nothing but to love and be loved. I sit here trembling, waiting for the night, waiting for that whining pimp Koos to come to my door again, and take everything I own from me in exchange for the key to her room.

I am not a courageous man, and I never have been: so I'm afraid of what may happen to me tonight. But I cannot go through life dreaming all the time, existing through the darkness on only a glimpse of heaven. Sooner or later, one has to gird one's loins (that's appropriate) and get up and find it. Even if it means giving away the world in exchange.

I probably make no sense. You're thinking, you who chanced on this testimony, you're thinking, who was he, this imbecile?

My name was Oliver Vassi. I am now thirty-eight years old. I was lawyer, until a year or more ago, when I began the search that ends tonight with that pimp and that key and that holy of holies.

But the story begins more than a year ago. It is many years since Jacqueline Ess first came to me.

She arrived out of the blue at my offices, claiming to be the widow of a friend of mine from Law School, one Benjamin Ess, and when I thought back, I remembered the face. A mutual friend who'd been at the wedding had shown me a photograph of Ben and his blushing bride. And here she was, every bit as elusive a beauty as her photograph promised.

I remember being acutely embarrassed at that first interview. She'd arrived at a busy time, and I was up to my neck in work. But I was so enthralled by her, I let all the day's interviews fall by the wayside, and when my secretary came in she gave me one of her steely glances as if to throw a bucket of cold water over me. I suppose I was enamored from the start, and she sensed the electric atmosphere in my office. Me, I pretended I was merely being polite to the widow of an old friend. I didn't like to think about passion: it wasn't a part of my nature, or so I thought. How little we know—I mean *really* know—about our capabilities.

Jacqueline told me lies at that first meeting. About how Ben had died of cancer, of how often he had spoken of me, and how fondly. I suppose she could have told me the truth then and there, and I would have lapped it up—I believe I was utterly devoted from the beginning.

But it's difficult to remember quite how and when interest in another human being flares into something more committed, more passionate. It may be that I am inventing the impact she had on me at that first meeting, simply re-inventing history to justify my later excesses. I'm not sure. Anyway, wherever and whenever it happened, however quickly or slowly, I succumbed to her, and the affair began.

I'm not a particularly inquisitive man where my friends, or my bed-partners, are concerned. As a lawyer one spends one's time going through the dirt of other people's lives, and frankly, eight hours a day of that is quite enough for me. When I'm out of the office my pleasure is in letting people be. I don't pry. I don't dig, I just take them on face value.

Jacqueline was no exception to this rule. She was a woman I was glad to have in my life whatever the truth of her past. She possessed a marvellous *sang-froid,* she was witty, bawdy, oblique. I had never met a more enchanting woman. It was none of my business how she'd lived with Ben, what the marriage had been like etc.,

etc. That was her history. I was happy to live in the present, and let the past die its own death. I think I even flattered myself that whatever pain she had experienced, I could help her forget it.

Certainly her stories had holes in them. As a lawyer, I was trained to be eagle-eyed where fabrications were concerned, and however much I tried to put my perceptions aside I sensed that she wasn't quite coming clean with me. But everyone has secrets: I knew that. Let her have hers, I thought.

Only once did I challenge her on a detail of her pretended life-story. In talking about Ben's death, she let slip that he had got what he deserved. I asked her what she meant. She smiled, that Gioconda smile of hers, and told me that she felt there was a balance to be redressed between men and women. I let the observation pass. After all, I was obsessed by that time, past all hope of salvation; whatever argument she was putting, I was happy to concede it.

She was so beautiful, you see. Not in any two-dimensional sense: she wasn't young, she wasn't innocent, she didn't have that pristine symmetry so favored by ad-men and photographers. Her face was plainly that of a woman in her early forties: it had been used to laugh and cry, and usage leaves its marks. But she had a power to transform herself, in the subtlest way, making that face as various as the sky. Early on, I thought it was a make-up trick. But as we slept together more and more, and I watched her in the mornings, sleep in her eyes, and in the evenings, heavy with fatigue, I soon realized she wore nothing on her skull but flesh and blood. What transformed her was internal: it was a trick of the will.

And, you know, that made me love her all the more.

Then one night I woke with her sleeping beside me. We slept often on the floor, which she preferred to the bed. Beds, she said, reminded her of marriage. Anyway, that night she was lying under a quilt on the carpet of my room, and I, simply out of adoration, was watching her face in sleep.

If one has given oneself utterly, watching the beloved sleep can be a vile experience. Perhaps some of you have known that paralysis, staring down at features closed to your enquiry, locked away from you where you can never, ever go, into the other's mind. As I say, for us who have given ourselves, that is a horror. One knows, in those moments, that one does not exist, except in relation to that face, that personality. Therefore, when that face is closed down, that personality is lost in its own unknowable world, one feels completely without purpose. A planet without a sun, revolving in darkness.

That's how I felt that night, looking down at her extraordinary features, and as I chewed on my soullessness, her face began to alter. She was clearly dreaming; but what dreams must she have been having. Her very fabric was on the move, her muscle, her hair, the down on her cheek moving to the dictates of some internal tide. Her lips bloomed from her bone, boiling up into a slavering tower of skin; her hair swirled around her head as though she were lying in water; the substance of her cheeks formed furrows and ridges like the ritual scars on a warrior; inflamed and throbbing patterns of tissue, swelling up and changing again even as a pattern formed. This fluxion was a terror to me, and I must have made some noise. She didn't wake, but came a little closer to the surface of sleep, leaving the deeper waters where these powers were sourced. The patterns sank away in an instant, and her face was again that of a gently sleeping woman.

That was, you can understand, a pivotal experience, even though I spent the next few days trying to convince myself that I hadn't seen it.

The effort was useless. I knew there was something wrong with her; and at that time I was certain she knew nothing about it. I was convinced that something in her system was awry, and that I was best to investigate her history before I told her what I had seen.

On reflection, of course, that seems laughably naïve. To think she wouldn't have known that she contained such a power. But it was easier for me to picture her as prey to such skill, than mistress of it. That's a man speaking of a woman; not just me, Oliver Vassi, of her, Jacqueline Ess. We cannot believe, we men, that power will ever reside happily in the body of a woman, unless that power is a male child. Not true power. The power must be in male hands, God-given. That's what our fathers tell us, idiots that they are.

Anyway, I investigated Jacqueline, as surreptitiously as I could. I had a contact in York where the couple had lived, and it wasn't difficult to get some enquiries moving. It took a week for my contact to get back to me, because he'd had to cut through a good deal of shit from the police to get a hint of the truth, but the news came, and it was bad.

Ben was dead, that much was true. But there was no way he had died of cancer. My contact had only got the vaguest clues as to the condition of Ben's corpse, but he gathered it had been spectacularly mutilated. And the prime suspect? My beloved Jacqueline Ess. The same innocent woman who was occupying my flat, sleeping by my side every night.

So I put it to her that she was hiding something from me. I don't know what I was expecting in return. What I got was a demonstration of her power. She gave it freely, without malice, but I would have been a fool not to have read a warning into it. She told me first how she had discovered her unique control over the sum and substance of human beings. In her despair, she said, when she was on the verge of killing herself, she had found, in the very deep-water trenches of her nature, faculties she had never known existed. Powers which came up out of those regions as she recovered, like fish to the light.

Then she showed me the smallest measure of these powers, plucking hairs from my head, one by one. Only a dozen; just to demonstrate her formidable skills. I felt them going. She just said: one from behind your ear, and I'd feel my skin creep and then jump as fingers of her volition snatched a hair out. Then another, and another. It was an incredible display; she had this power down to a fine art, locating and withdrawing single hairs from my scalp with the precision of tweezers.

Frankly, I was sitting there rigid with fear, knowing that she was just toying with me. Sooner or later, I was certain the time would be right for her to silence me permanently.

But she had doubts about herself. She told me how the skill, though she had honed it, scared her. She needed, she said, someone to teach her how to use it best. And I was not that somebody. I was just a man who loved her, who had loved her before this revelation, and would love her still, in spite of it.

In fact, after that display I quickly came to accommodate a new vision of Jacqueline. Instead of fearing her, I became more devoted to this woman who tolerated my possession of her body.

My work became an irritation, a distraction that came between me and thinking of my beloved. What reputation I had began to deteriorate; I lost briefs, I lost credibility. In the space of two or three months my professional life dwindled away to almost nothing. Friends despaired of me, colleagues avoided me.

It wasn't that she was feeding on me. I want to be clear about that. She was no lamia, no succubus. What happened to me, my fall from grace with ordinary life if you like, was of my own making. She didn't bewitch me; that's a romantic lie to excuse rape. She was a sea: and I had to swim in her. Does that make any sense? I'd lived my life on the shore, in the solid world of law, and I was tired of it. She was liquid; a boundless sea in a single body, a deluge in a small room, and I will gladly drown in her, if she grants me the chance. But that was my decision. Understand that. This has always been my decision. I have decided to go to the room tonight, and be with her one final time. That is of my own free will.

And what man would not? She was (is) sublime.

For a month after that demonstration of power I lived in a permanent ecstasy of her. When I was with her she showed me ways to love beyond the limits of any other creature on God's earth. I say beyond the limits: with her there were no limits. And when I was away from her the reverie continued: because she seemed to have changed my world.

Then she left me.

I knew why: she'd gone to find someone to teach her how to use strength. But understanding her reasons made it no easier.

I broke down: lost my job, lost my identity, lost the few friends I had left in the world. I scarcely noticed. They were minor losses, beside the loss of Jacqueline . . ."

"Jacqueline."

My God, she thought, can this really be the most influential man in the country? He looked so unprepossessing, so very unspectacular. His chin wasn't even strong.

But Titus Pettifer was power.

He ran more monopolies than he could count; his word in the financial world could break companies like sticks, destroying the ambitions of hundreds, the careers of thousands. Fortunes were made overnight in his shadow, entire corporations fell when he blew on them, casualties of his whim. This man knew power if any man knew it. He had to be learned from.

"You wouldn't mind if I called you J., would you?"

"No."

"Have you been waiting long?"

"Long enough."

"I don't normally leave beautiful women waiting."

"Yes you do."

She knew him already: two minutes in his presence was enough to find his measure. He would come quickest to her if she was quietly insolent.

"Do you always call women you've never met before by their initials?"

"It's convenient for filing; do you mind?"

"It depends."

"On what?"

"What I get in return for giving you the privilege."

"It's a privilege, is it, to know your name?"

"Yes."

"Well . . . I'm flattered. Unless of course you grant that privilege widely?"

She shook her head. No, he could see she wasn't profligate with her affections.

"Why have you waited so long to see me?" he said. "Why have I had reports of your wearing my secretaries down with your constant demands to meet with me? Do you want money? Because if you do you'll go away empty-handed. I became rich by being mean, and the richer I get, the meaner I become."

The remark was truth; he spoke it plainly.

"I don't want money," she said, equally plainly.

"That's refreshing."

"There's richer than you."

He raised his eyebrows in surprise. She could bite, this beauty.

"True," he said. There were at least half a dozen richer men in the hemisphere.

"I'm not an adoring little nobody. I haven't come here to screw a name. I've come here because we can be together. We have a great deal to offer each other."

"Such as?" he said.

"I have my body."

He smiled. It was the straightest offer he'd heard in years.

"And what do I offer you in return for such largesse?"

"I want to learn—"

"Learn?"

"—how to use power."

She was stranger and stranger, this one.

"What do you mean?" he replied, playing for time. He hadn't got the measure of her; she vexed him, confounded him.

"Shall I recite it for you again, in bourgeois?" she said, playing insolence with such a smile he almost felt attractive again.

"No need. You want to learn to use power. I suppose I could teach you—"

"I know you can."

"You realize I'm a married man. Virginia and I have been together eighteen years."

"You have three sons, four houses, a maid-servant called Mirabelle. You loathe New York, and you love Bangkok; your shirt collar is 16½, your favorite color green."

"Turquoise."

"You're getting subtler in your old age."

"I'm not old."

"Eighteen years a married man. It ages you prematurely."

"Not me."

"Prove it."

"How?"

"Take me."

"What?"

"Take me."

"Here?"

"Draw the blinds, lock the door, turn off the computer terminus, and take me. I dare you."

"Dare?"

How long was it since anyone had *dared* him to do anything?

"Dare?"

He was excited. He hadn't been so excited in a dozen

years. He drew the blinds, locked the door, turned off
the video display of his fortunes.

My God, she thought, I've got him.

It wasn't an easy passion, not like that with Vassi. For
one thing, Pettifer was a clumsy, uncultured lover. For
another, he was too nervous of his wife to be a wholly
successful adulterer. He thought he saw Virginia everywhere: in the lobbies of the hotels they took a room in
for the afternoon, in cabs cruising the street outside
their rendezvous, once even (he swore the likeness was
exact) dressed as a waitress, and swabbing down a table
in a restaurant. All fictional fears, but they dampened
the spontaneity of the romance somewhat.

Still, she was learning from him. He was as brilliant a
potentate as he was inept a lover. She learned how to be
powerful without exercising power, how to keep one's
self uncontaminated by the foulness all charisma stirs
up in the uncharismatic; how to make the plain deci-
sions plainly; how to be merciless. Not that she needed
much education in that particular quarter. Perhaps it
was more truthful to say he taught her never to regret
her absence of instinctive compassion, but to judge with
her intellect alone who deserved extinction and who
might be numbered amongst the righteous.

Not once did she show herself to him, though she
used her skills in the most secret of ways to tease pleasure out of his stale nerves.

In the fourth week of their affair they were lying side
by side in a lilac room, while the mid-afternoon traffic
growled in the street below. It had been a bad bout of
sex; he was nervous, and no tricks would coax him out
of himself. It was over quickly, almost without heat.

He was going to tell her something. She knew it: it
was waiting, this revelation, somewhere at the back of
his throat. Turning to him she massaged his temples
with her mind, and soothed him into speech.

He was about to spoil the day.

He was about to spoil his career.

He was about, God help him, to spoil his life.

"I have to stop seeing you," he said.

He wouldn't dare, she thought.

"I'm not sure what I know about you, or rather, what I *think* I know about you, but it makes me . . . cautious of you, J. Do you understand?"

"No."

"I'm afraid I suspect you of . . . crimes."

"Crimes?"

"You have a history."

"Who's been rooting?" she asked. "Surely not Virginia?"

"No, not Virginia, she's beyond curiosity."

"Who then?"

"It's not your business."

"Who?"

She pressed lightly on his temples. It hurt him and he winced.

"What's wrong?" she asked.

"My head's aching."

"Tension, that's all, just tension. I can take it away, Titus." She touched her finger to his forehead, relaxing her hold on him. He sighed as relief came.

"Is that better?"

"Yes."

"Who's been snooping, Titus?"

"I have a personal secretary. Lyndon. You've heard me speak of him. He knew about our relationship from the beginning. Indeed, he books the hotels, arranges my cover stories for Virginia."

There was a sort of boyishness in this speech, that was rather touching. As though he was embarrassed to leave her, rather than heartbroken. "Lyndon's quite a miracle worker. He's maneuvered a lot of things to make it easier between us. So he's got nothing against you. It's just that he happened to see one of the photographs I took of you. I gave them to him to shred."

"Why?"

"I shouldn't have taken them; it was a mistake. Virginia might have . . ." He paused, began again. "Anyhow, he recognized you, although he couldn't remember where he'd seen you before."

"But he remembered eventually."

"He used to work for one of my newspapers, as a gossip columnist. That's how he came to be my personal assistant. He remembered you from your previous incarnation, as it were. Jacqueline Ess, the wife of Benjamin Ess, deceased."

"Deceased."

"He brought me some other photographs, not as pretty as the ones of you."

"Photographs of what?"

"Your home. And the body of your husband. They said it was a body, though in God's name there was precious little human being left in it."

"There was precious little to start with," she said simply, thinking of Ben's cold eyes, and colder hands. Fit only to be shut up, and forgotten.

"What happened?"

"To Ben? He was killed."

"How?" Did his voice waver a little?

"Very easily." She had risen from the bed, and was standing by the window. Strong summer light carved its way through the slats of the blind, ridges of shadow and sunlight charting the contours of her face.

"You did it."

"Yes." He had taught her to be plain. "Yes, I did it."

He had taught her an economy of threat too. "Leave me, and I'll do the same again."

He shook his head. "Never. You wouldn't dare."

He was standing in front of her now.

"We must understand each other, J. I am powerful and I am pure. Do you see? My public face isn't even touched by a glimmer of scandal. I could afford a mistress, a dozen mistresses, to be revealed. But a murderess? No, that would spoil my life."

"Is he blackmailing you? This Lyndon?"

He stared at the day through the blinds, with a crippled look on his face. There was a twitch in the nerves of his cheek, under his left eye.

"Yes, if you must know," he said in a dead voice. "The bastard has me for all I'm worth."

"I see."

"And if he can guess, so can others. You understand?"

"I'm strong: you're strong. We can twist them around our little fingers."

"No."

"Yes! I have skills, Titus."

"I don't want to know."

"You *will* know," she said.

She looked at him, taking hold of his hands without touching him. He watched, all astonished eyes, as his unwilling hands were raised to touch her face, to stroke her hair with the fondest of gestures. She made him run his trembling fingers across her breasts, taking them with more ardor than he could summon on his own initiative.

"You are always too tentative, Titus," she said, making him paw her almost to the point of bruising. "This is how I like it." Now his hands were lower, fetching out a different look from her face. Tides were moving over it, she was all alive—

"Deeper—"

His finger intruded, his thumb stroked.

"I like that, Titus. Why can't you do that to me without me demanding?"

He blushed. He didn't like to talk about what they did together. She coaxed him deeper, whispering.

"I won't break, you know. Virginia may be Dresden china, I'm not. I want feeling; I want something that I can remember you by when I'm not with you. Nothing is everlasting, is it? But I want something to keep me warm through the night."

He was sinking to his knees, his hands kept, by her design, on her and in her, still roving like two lustful crabs. His body was awash with sweat. It was, she thought, the first time she'd ever seen him sweat.

"Don't kill me," he whimpered.

"I could wipe you out." Wipe, she thought, then put the image out of her mind before she did him some harm.

"I know. I know," he said. "You can kill me easily."

He was crying. My God, she thought, the great man is at my feet, sobbing like a baby. What can I learn of power from this puerile performance? She plucked the tears off his cheeks, using rather more strength than the task required. His skin reddened under her gaze.

"Let me be, J. I can't help you. I'm useless to you."

It was true. He was absolutely useless. Contemptuously, she let his hands go. They fell limply by his sides.

"Don't ever try and find me, Titus. You understand? Don't ever send your minions after me to preserve your reputation, because I will be more merciless than you've ever been."

He said nothing; just knelt there, facing the window, while she washed her face, drank the coffee they'd ordered, and left.

Lyndon was surprised to find the door of his office ajar. It was only seven-thirty-six. None of the secretaries would be in for another hour. Clearly one of the cleaners had been remiss, leaving the door unlocked. He'd find out who: sack her.

He pushed the door open.

Jacqueline was sitting with her back to the door. He recognized the back of her head, that fall of auburn hair. A sluttish display; too teased, too wild. His office, an annex to Mr. Pettifer's, was kept meticulously ordered. He glanced over it: everything seemed to be in place.

"What are you doing here?"

She took a little breath, preparing herself.

This was the first time she had planned to do it. Before it had been a spur-of-the-moment decision.

He was approaching the desk, and putting down his briefcase and his neatly-folded copy of the *Financial Times*.

"You have no right to come in here without my permission," he said.

She turned on the lazy swivel of his chair; the way he did when he had people in to discipline.

"Lyndon," she said.

"Nothing you can say or do will change the facts, Mrs. Ess," he said, saving her the trouble of introducing the subject, "you are a cold-blooded killer. It was my bounden duty to inform Mr. Pettifer of the situation."

"You did it for the good of Titus?"

"Of course."

"And the blackmail, that was also for the good of Titus, was it?"

"Get out of my office—"

"Was it, Lyndon?"

"You're a whore! Whores know nothing: they are ignorant, diseased animals," he spat. "Oh, you're cunning, I grant you that—but then so's any slut with a living to make."

She stood up. He expected a riposte. He got none; at least not verbally. But he felt a tautness across his face: as though someone was pressing on it.

"What . . . are . . . you . . . doing?" he asked.

"Doing?"

His eyes were being forced into slits like a child imitating a monstrous Oriental, his mouth was hauled wide and tight, his smile brilliant. The words were difficult to say—

"Stop . . . it . . ."

She shook her head.

"Whore . . ." he said again, still defying her.

She just stared at him. His face was beginning to jerk

and twitch under the pressure, the muscles going into spasm.

"The police . . ." he tried to say, "if you lay a finger on me . . ."

"I won't," she said, and pressed home her advantage.

Beneath his clothes he felt the same tension all over his body, pulling his skin, drawing him tighter and tighter. Something was going to give; he knew it. Some part of him would be weak, and tear under this relentless assault. And if he once began to break open, nothing would prevent her ripping him apart. He worked all this out quite coolly, while his body twitched and he swore at her through his enforced grin.

"Cunt," he said. "Syphilitic cunt."

He didn't seem to be afraid, she thought.

In extremis he just unleashed so much hatred of her, the fear was entirely eclipsed. Now he was calling her a whore again; though his face was distorted almost beyond recognition.

And then he began to split.

The tear began at the bridge of his nose and ran up, across his brow, and down, bisecting his lips and his chin, then his neck and chest. In a matter of seconds his shirt was dyed red, his dark suit darkening further, his cuffs and trouser-legs pouring blood. The skin flew off his hands like gloves off a surgeon, and two rings of scarlet tissue lolled down to either side of his flayed face like the ears of an elephant.

His name-calling had stopped.

He had been dead of shock now for ten seconds, though she was still working him over vengefully, tugging his skin off his body and flinging the scraps around the room, until at last he stood, steaming, in his red suit, and his red shirt, and his shiny red shoes, and looked, to her eyes, a little more like a sensitive man. Content with the effect, she released him. He lay down quietly in a blood puddle and slept.

My God, she thought, as she calmly took the stairs

out the back way, that was murder in the first degree.

She saw no reports of the death in any of the papers, and nothing on the news bulletins. Lyndon had apparently died as he had lived, hidden from public view.

But she knew wheels, so big their hubs could not be seen by insignificant individuals like herself, would be moving. What they would do, how they would change her life, she could only guess at. But the murder of Lyndon had not simply been spite, though that had been a part of it. No, she'd also wanted to stir them up, her enemies in the world, and bring them after her. Let them show their hands: let them show their contempt, their terror. She'd gone through her life, it seemed, looking for a sign of herself, only able to define her nature by the look in others' eyes. Now she wanted an end to that. It was time to deal with her pursuers.

Surely now everyone who had seen her, Pettifer first, then Vassi, would come after her, and she would close their eyes permanently: make them forgetful of her. Only then, the witnesses destroyed, would she be free.

Pettifer didn't come, of course, not in person. It was easy for him to find agents, men without scruple or compassion, but with a nose for pursuit that would shame a bloodhound.

A trap was being laid for her, though she couldn't yet see its jaws. There were signs of it everywhere. An eruption of birds from behind a wall, a peculiar light from a distant window, footsteps, whistles, dark-suited men reading the news at the limit of her vision. As the weeks passed they didn't come any closer to her, but then neither did they go away. They waited, like cats in a tree, their tails twitching, their eyes lazy.

But the pursuit had Pettifer's mark. She'd learned enough from him to recognize his circumspection and his guile. They would come for her eventually, not in her time, but in theirs. Perhaps not even in theirs: in his. And though she never saw his face, it was as though

Titus was on her heels personally.

My God, she thought, I'm in danger of my life and I don't care.

It was useless, this power over flesh, if it had no direction behind it. She had used it for her own petty reasons, for the gratification of nervous pleasure and sheer anger. But these displays hadn't brought her any closer to other people: they just made her a freak in their eyes.

Sometimes she thought of Vassi, and wondered where he was, what he was doing. He hadn't been a strong man, but he'd had a little passion in his soul. More than Ben, more than Pettifer, certainly more than Lyndon. And, she remembered, fondly, he was the only man she'd ever known who called her Jacqueline. All the rest had manufactured unendearing corruptions of her name: Jackie, or J., or, in Ben's more irritating moods, Ju-ju. Only Vassi had called her Jacqueline, plain and simple, accepting, in his formal way, the completeness of her, the totality of her. And when she thought of him, tried to picture how he might return to her, she feared for him.

Vassi's Testimony (part two)

Of course I searched for her. It's only when you've lost someone, you realize the nonsense of that phrase "it's a small world." It isn't. It's a vast, devouring world, especially if you're alone.

When I was a lawyer, locked in that incestuous coterie, I used to see the same faces day after day. Some I'd exchange words with, some smiles, some nods. We belonged, even if we were enemies at the Bar, to the same complacent circle. We ate at the same tables, we drank elbow to elbow. We even shared mistresses, though we didn't always know it at the time. In such circumstances, it's easy to believe the world means you no harm. Certainly you grow older, but then so does everyone else. You even believe, in your self-satisfied way, that the passage of years makes you a little wiser. Life is bearable; even the 3 a.m. sweats come more infrequently as the bank-balance swells.

But to think that the world is harmless is to lie to yourself, to believe in so-called certainties that are, in fact, simply shared delusions.

When she left, all the delusions fell away, and all the lies I had assiduously lived by became strikingly apparent.

It's not a small world, when there's only one face in it you can bear to look upon, and that face is lost somewhere in a maelstrom. It's not a small world when the few, vital memories of your object of affection are in danger of being trampled out by the thousands of moments that assail you every day, like children tugging at you, demanding your sole attention.

I was a broken man.

I would find myself (there's an apt phrase) sleeping in tiny bedrooms in forlorn hotels, drinking more often than eating, and writing her name, like a classic obsessive, over and over again. On the walls, on the pillow, on the palm of my hand. I broke the skin of my palm with my pen, and the ink infected it. The mark's still there, I'm looking at it now. Jacqueline it says. Jacqueline.

Then one day, entirely by chance, I saw her. It sounds melodramatic, but I thought I was going to die at that moment. I'd imagined her for so long, keyed myself up for seeing her again, that when it happened I felt my limbs weaken, and I was sick in the middle of the street. Not a classic reunion. The lover, on seeing his beloved, throws up down his shirt. But then, nothing that happened between Jacqueline and myself was ever quite normal. Or natural.

I followed her, which was difficult. There were crowds, and she was walking fast. I didn't know whether to call out her name or not. I decided not. What would she have done anyway, seeing this unshaven lunatic shambling towards her, calling her name? She would have run probably. Or worse, she would have reached into my chest, seizing my heart in her will, and put me out of my misery before I could reveal her to the world.

So I was silent, and simply followed her, doggedly, to what I assumed was her apartment. And I stayed there, or in the vicinity, for the next two and a half days, not quite knowing what to do. It was a ridiculous dilemma. After all this time of watching for her, now that she was within speaking distance, touching distance, I didn't dare approach.

Maybe I feared death. But then, here I am, in this stinking room in Amsterdam, setting my testimony down and waiting for Koos to bring me her key, and I don't fear death now. Probably it was my vanity that prevented me from approaching her. I didn't want her to see me cracked and desolate; I wanted to come to her clean, her dream-lover.

While I waited, they came for her.

I don't know who they were. Two men, plainly dressed. I don't think policemen: too smooth. Cultured even. And she didn't resist. She went smilingly, as if to the opera.

At the first opportunity I returned to the building a little better dressed, located her apartment from the porter, and broke in. She had been living plainly. In one corner of the room she had set up a table, and had been writing her memoirs. I sat down and read, and eventually took the pages away with me. She had got no further than the first seven years of her life. I wondered, again in my vanity, if I would have been chronicled in the book. Probably not.

I took some of her clothes too; only items she had worn when I had known her. And nothing intimate: I'm not a fetishist. I wasn't going to go home and bury my face in the smell of her underwear. But I wanted something to remember her by; to picture her in. Though on reflection I never met a human being more fitted to dress purely in her skin.

So I lost her a second time, more the fault of my own

cowardice than circumstance.

Pettifer didn't come near the house they were keeping
Mrs. Ess in for four weeks. She was given more or less
everything she asked for, except her freedom, and she
only asked for that in the most abstracted fashion. She
wasn't interested in escape: though it would have been
easy to achieve. Once or twice she wondered if Titus had
told the two men and the woman who were keeping her
a prisoner in the house exactly what she was capable of:
she guessed not. They treated her as though she were
simply a woman Titus had set eyes on and desired. They
had procured her for his bed, simple as that.

With a room to herself, and an endless supply of
paper, she began to write her memoirs again, from the
beginning.

It was late summer, and the nights were getting chilly.
Sometimes, to warm herself, she would lie on the floor
(she'd asked them to remove the bed) and will her body
to ripple like the surface of a lake. Her body, without
sex, became a mystery to her again; and she realized for
the first time that physical love had been an exploration
of that most intimate, and yet most unknown region of
her being: her flesh. She had understood herself best
embracing someone else: seen her own substance clearly
only when another's lips were laid on it, adoring and
gentle. She thought of Vassi again; and the lake, at the
thought of him, was roused as if by a tempest. Her
breasts shook into curling mountains, her belly ran with
extraordinary tides, currents crossed and recrossed her
flickering face, lapping at her mouth and leaving their
mark like waves on sand. As she was fluid in his memory, so as she remembered him, she liquified.

She thought of the few times she had been at peace in
her life; and physical love, discharging ambition and
vanity, had always preceded those fragile moments.
There were other ways presumably; but her experience
had been limited. Her mother had always said that

women, being more at peace with themselves than men, needed fewer distractions from their hurts. But she'd not found it like that at all. She'd found her life full of hurts, but almost empty of ways to salve them.

She left off writing her memoirs when she reached her ninth year. She despaired of telling her story from that point on, with the first realization of on-coming puberty. She burnt the papers on a bonfire she lit in the middle of her room the day that Pettifer arrived.

My God, she thought, this can't be power.

Pettifer looked sick; as physically changed as a friend she'd lost to cancer. One month seemingly healthy, the next sucked up from the inside, self-devoured. He looked like a husk of a man: his skin grey and mottled. Only his eyes glittered, and those like the eyes of a mad dog.

He was dressed immaculately, as though for a wedding.

"J."

"Titus."

He looked her up and down.

"Are you well?"

"Thank you, yes."

"They give you everything you ask for?"

"Perfect hosts."

"You haven't resisted."

"Resisted?"

"Being here. Locked up. I was prepared, after Lyndon, for another slaughter of the innocents."

"Lyndon was not innocent, Titus. These people are. You didn't tell them."

"I didn't deem it necessary. May I close the door?"

He was her captor: but he came like an emissary to the camp of a greater power. She liked the way he was with her, cowed but elated. He closed the door, and locked it.

"I love you, J. And I fear you. In fact, I think I love you because I fear you. Is that a sickness?"

"I would have thought so."

"Yes, so would I."

"Why did you take such a time to come?"

"I had to put my affairs in order. Otherwise there would have been chaos. When I was gone."

"You're leaving?"

He looked into her, the muscles of his face ruffled by anticipation.

"I hope so."

"Where to?"

Still she didn't guess what had brought him to the house, his affairs neatened, his wife unknowingly asked forgiveness of as she slept, all channels of escape closed, all contradictions laid to rest.

Still she didn't guess he'd come to die.

"I'm reduced by you, J. Reduced to nothing. And there is nowhere for me to go. Do you follow?"

"No."

"I cannot live without you," he said. The cliché was unpardonable. Could he not have found a better way to say it? She almost laughed, it was so trite.

But he hadn't finished.

"—and I certainly can't live *with* you." Abruptly, the tone changed. "Because you revolt me, woman, your whole being disgusts me."

"So?" she asked, softly.

"So . . ." He was tender again and she began to understand. ". . . kill me."

It was grotesque. The glittering eyes were steady on her.

"It's what I want," he said. "Believe me, it's all I want in the world. Kill me, however you please. I'll go without resistance, without complaint."

She remembered the old joke. Masochist to Sadist: Hurt me! For God's sake, hurt me! Sadist to Masochist: No.

"And if I refuse?" she said.

"You can't refuse. I'm loathsome."

"But I don't hate you, Titus."

"You should. I'm weak. I'm useless to you. I taught you nothing."

"You taught me a great deal. I can control myself now."

"Lyndon's death was controlled, was it?"

"Certainly."

"It looked a little excessive to me."

"He got everything he deserved."

"Give me what I deserve, then, in my turn. I've locked you up. I've rejected you when you needed me. Punish me for it."

"I survived."

"J!"

Even in this extremity he couldn't call her by her full name.

"Please to God. Please to God. I need only this one thing from you. Do it out of whatever motive you have in you. Compassion, or contempt, or love. But do it, please do it."

"No," she said.

He crossed the room suddenly, and slapped her, very hard.

"Lyndon said you were a whore. He was right; you are. Gutterslut, nothing better."

He walked away, turned, walked back, hit her again, faster, harder, and again, six or seven times, backwards and forwards.

Then he stopped, panting.

"You want money?" Bargains now. Blows, then bargains.

She was seeing him twisted through tears of shock, which she was unable to prevent.

"Do you want money?" he said again.

"What do you think?"

He didn't hear her sarcasm, and began to scatter notes around her feet, dozens and dozens of them, like offerings around the Statue of the Virgin.

"Anything you want," he said, *"Jacqueline."*

In her belly she felt something close to pain as the urge to kill him found birth, but she resisted it. It was playing into his hands, becoming the instrument of his will: powerless. Usage again; that's all she ever got. She had been bred like a cow, to give a certain supply. Of care to husbands, of milk to babies, of death to old men. And, like a cow, she was expected to be compliant with every demand made of her, whenever the call came. Well, not this time.

She went to the door.

"Where are you going?"

She reached for the key.

"Your death is your own business, not mine," she said.

He ran at her before she could unlock the door, and the blow—in its force, in its malice—was totally unexpected.

"Bitch!" he shrieked, a hail of blows coming fast upon the first.

In her stomach, the thing that wanted to kill grew a little larger.

He had his fingers tangled in her hair, and pulled her back into the room, shouting obscenities at her, an endless stream of them, as though he'd opened a dam full of sewer-water on her. This was just another way for him to get what he wanted she told herself, if you succumb to this you've lost: he's just manipulating you. Still the words came: the same dirty words that had been thrown at generations of unsubmissive women. Whore; heretic; cunt; bitch; monster.

Yes, she was that.

Yes, she thought: monster I am.

The thought made it easy. She turned. He knew what she intended even before she looked at him. He dropped his hands from her head. Her anger was already in her throat coming out of her—crossing the air between them.

Monster he calls me: monster I am.

I do this for myself, not for him. Never for him. For myself!

He gasped as her will touched him, and the glittering eyes stopped glittering for a moment, the will to die became the will to survive, all too late of course, and he roared. She heard answering shouts, steps, threats on the stairs. They would be in the room in a matter of moments.

"You are an animal," she said.

"No," he said, certain even now that his place was in command.

"You don't exist," she said, advancing on him. "They'll never find the part that was Titus. Titus is gone. The rest is just—"

The pain was terrible. It stopped even a voice coming out from him. Or was that her again, changing his throat, his palate, his very head? She was unlocking the plates of his skull, and reorganizing him.

No, he wanted to say, this isn't the subtle ritual I had planned. I wanted to die folded into you, I wanted to go with my mouth clamped to yours, cooling in you as I died. This is not the way I want it.

No. No. No.

They were at the door, the men who'd kept her here, beating on it. She had no fear of them, of course, except that they might spoil her handiwork before the final touches were added to it.

Someone was hurling themselves at the door now. Wood splintered: the door was flung open. The two men were both armed. They pointed their weapons at her, steady-handed.

"Mr. Pettifer?" said the younger man. In the corner of the room, under the table, Pettifer's eyes shone.

"Mr. Pettifer?" he said again, forgetting the woman.

Pettifer shook his snouted head. Don't come any closer, please, he thought.

The man crouched down and stared under the table

at the disgusting beast that was squatting there; bloody
from its transformation, but alive. She had killed his
nerves: he felt no pain. He just survived, his hands
knotted into paws, his legs scooped up around his back,
knees broken so he had the look of a four-legged crab,
his brain exposed, his eyes lidless, lower jaw broken and
swept up over his top jaw like a bulldog, ears torn off,
spine snapped, humanity bewitched into another state.

"You are an animal," she'd said. It wasn't a bad fac-
simile of beasthood.

The man with the gun gagged as he recognized
fragments of his master. He stood up, greasy-chinned,
and glanced around at the woman.

Jacqueline shrugged.

"You did this?" Awe mingled with the revulsion.

She nodded.

"Come Titus," she said, clicking her fingers.

The beast shook its head, sobbing.

"Come Titus," she said more forcefully, and Titus
Pettifer waddled out of his hiding place, leaving a trail
like a punctured meat-sack.

The man fired at Pettifer's remains out of sheer instinct. Anything, anything at all to prevent this disgusting creature from approaching him.

Titus stumbled two steps back on his bloody paws,
shook himself as if to dislodge the death in him, and
failing, died.

"Content?" she asked.

The gunman looked up from the execution. Was the
power talking to him? No; Jacqueline was staring at
Pettifer's corpse, asking the question of him.

Content?

The gunman dropped his weapon. The other man did
the same.

"How did this happen?" asked the man at the door.
A simple question: a child's question.

"He asked," said Jacqueline. "It was all I could give
him."

The gunman nodded, and fell to his knees.

Vassi's Testimony (final part)

Chance has played a worryingly large part in my romance with Jacqueline Ess. Sometimes it's seemed I've been subject to every tide that passes through the world, spun around by the merest flick of accident's wrist. Other times I've had the suspicion that she was masterminding my life, as she was the lives of a hundred others, a thousand others, arranging every fluke meeting, choreographing my victories and my defeats, escorting me, blindly, towards this last encounter.

I found her without knowing I'd found her, that was the irony of it. I'd traced her first to a house in Surrey, a house that had a year previous seen the murder of one Titus Pettifer, a billionaire shot by one of his own bodyguards. In the upstairs room, where the murder had taken place, all was serenity. If she had been there, they had removed any sign. But the house, now in virtual ruin, was prey to all manner of graffiti; and on the stained plaster wall of that room someone had scrawled a woman. She was obscenely over-endowed, her gaping sex blazing with what looked like lightning. And at her feet there was a creature of indeterminate species. Perhaps a crab, perhaps a dog, perhaps even a man. Whatever it was it had no power over itself. It sat in the light of her agonizing presence and counted itself amongst the fortunate. Looking at that wizened creature, with its eyes turned up to gaze on the burning Madonna, I knew the picture was a portrait of Jacqueline.

I don't know how long I stood looking at the graffiti, but I was interrupted by a man who looked to be in a worse condition than me. A beard that had never been trimmed or washed, a frame so wasted I wondered how he managed to stand upright, and a smell that would not have shamed a skunk.

I never knew his name: but he was, he told me, the maker of the picture on the wall. It was easy to believe that. His desperation, his hunger, his confusion were all marks of a man who had seen Jacqueline.

If I was rough in my interrogation of him I'm sure he forgave me. It was an unburdening for him, to tell everything he'd seen the day that Pettifer had been killed, and know that I believed it all. He told me his fellow bodyguard, the man who had fired the shots that had killed Pettifer, had committed suicide in prison.

His life, he said, was meaningless. She had destroyed it. I gave him what reassurances I could; that she meant no harm, and that he needn't fear that she would come for him. When I told him that, he cried, more, I think, out of loss than relief.

Finally I asked him if he knew where Jacqueline was now. I'd left that question to the end, though it had been the most pressing enquiry, because I suppose I didn't dare hope he'd know. But my God, he did. She had not left the house immediately after the shooting of Pettifer. She had sat down with this man, and talked to him quietly about his children, his tailor, his car. She'd asked him what his mother had been like, and he'd told her his mother had been a prostitute. Had she been happy? Jacqueline had asked. He'd said he didn't know. Did she ever cry, she'd asked. He'd said he never saw her laugh or cry in his life. And she'd nodded, and thanked him.

Later, before his suicide, the other gunman had told him Jacqueline had gone to Amsterdam. This he knew for a fact, from a man called Koos. And so the circle begins to close, yes?

I was in Amsterdam seven weeks, without finding a single clue to her whereabouts, until yesterday evening. Seven weeks of celibacy, which is unusual for me. Listless with frustration I went down to the red-light district, to find a woman. They sit there you know, in the windows, like mannequins, beside pink-fringed lamps. Some have miniature dogs on their laps; some read. Most just stare out at the street, as if mesmerized.

There were no faces there that interested me. They all seemed joyless, lightless, too much unlike her. Yet I couldn't leave. I was like a fat boy in a sweet shop, too nauseous to buy, too gluttonous to go.

Towards the middle of the night, I was spoken to out of the crowd by a young man who, on closer inspection, was not young at all, but heavily made up. He had no eyebrows, just pencil marks drawn on to his shiny skin. A cluster of gold earrings in his left ear, a half-eaten peach in his white-gloved hand, open sandals, lacquered toenails. He took hold of my sleeve, proprietorially.

I must have sneered at his sickening appearance, but he didn't seem at all upset by my contempt. You look like a man of discernment, he said. I looked nothing of the kind: you must be mistaken, I said. No, he replied, I am not mistaken. You are Oliver Vassi.

My first thought, absurdly, was that he intended to kill me. I tried to pull away; his grip on my cuff was relentless.

You want a woman, he said. Did I hesitate enough for him to know I meant yes, though I said no? I have a woman like no other, he went on, she's a miracle. I know you'll want to meet her in the flesh.

What made me know it was Jacqueline he was talking about? Perhaps the fact that he had known me from out of the crowd, as though she was up at a window somewhere, ordering her admirers to be brought to her like a diner ordering lobster from a tank. Perhaps too the way his eyes shone at me, meeting mine without fear because fear, like rapture, he felt only in the presence of one creature on God's cruel earth. Could I not also see myself reflected in his perilous look? He knew Jacqueline, I had no doubt of it.

He knew I was hooked, because once I hesitated he turned away from me with a mincing shrug, as if to say: you missed your chance. Where is she? I said, seizing his twig-thin arm. He cocked his head down the street and I followed him, suddenly as witless as an idiot, out of the throng. The road emptied as we walked; the red lights gave way to gloom, and then to darkness. If I asked him where we were going once I asked him a dozen times; he chose not to answer, until we reached a narrow door in a narrow house down some razor-thin street. We're here, he announced, as though the hovel were the Palace of Versailles.

Up two flights in the otherwise empty house there was a room with a black door. He pressed me to it. It was locked.

"See," he invited, "she's inside."

"It's locked," I replied. My heart was fit to burst: she was near, for certain, I knew she was near.

"See," he said again, and pointed to a tiny hole in the panel of the door. I devoured the light through it, pushing my eye towards her through the tiny hole.

The squalid interior was empty, except for a mattress and Jacqueline. She lay spreadeagled, her wrists and ankles bound to rough posts set in the bare floor at the four corners of the mattress.

"Who did this?" I demanded, not taking my eye from her nakedness.

"She asks," he replied. "It is her desire. She asks."

She had heard my voice; she cranked up her head with some difficulty and stared directly at the door. When she looked at me all the hairs rose on my head, I swear it, in welcome, and swayed at her command.

"Oliver," she said.

"Jacqueline." I pressed the word to the wood with a kiss.

Her body was seething, her shaved sex opening and closing like some exquisite plant, purple and lilac and rose.

"Let me in," I said to Koos.

"You will not survive one night with her."

"Let me in."

"She is expensive," he warned.

"How much do you want?"

"Everything you have. The shirt off your back, your money, your jewellery; then she is yours."

I wanted to beat the door down, or break his nicotine-stained fingers one by one until he gave me the key. He knew what I was thinking.

"The key is hidden," he said, "and the door is strong. You must pay, Mr. Vassi. You want to pay."

It was true. I wanted to pay.

"You want to give me all you have ever owned, all you have ever been. You want to go to her with nothing to claim you back. I know this. It's how they all go to her."

"All? Are there many?"

"She is insatiable," he said, without relish. It wasn't a pimp's boast: it was his pain, I saw that clearly. "I am always finding more for her, and burying them."

Burying them.

That, I suppose, is Koos' function; he disposes of the dead. And he will get his lacquered hands on me after tonight; he will fetch me off her when I am dry and useless to her, and find some pit, some canal, some furnace to lose me in. The thought isn't particularly attractive.

Yet here I am with all the money I could raise from selling my few remaining possessions on the table in front of me, my dignity gone, my life hanging on a thread, waiting for a pimp and a key.

It's well dark now, and he's late. But I think he is obliged to come. Not for the money, he probably has few requirements beyond his heroin and his mascara. He will come to do business with me because she demands it and he is in thrall to her, every bit as much as I am. Oh, he will come. Of course he will come.

Well, I think that is sufficient.

This is my testimony. I have no time to re-read it now. His footsteps are on the stairs (he limps) and I must go with him. This I leave to whoever finds it, to use as they think fit. By morning I shall be dead, and happy. Believe it.

•   •   •

My God, she thought, Koos has cheated me.

Vassi had been outside the door, she'd felt his flesh with her mind and she'd embraced it. But Koos hadn't let him in, despite her explicit orders. Of all men, Vassi was to be allowed free access, Koos knew that. But he'd cheated her, the way they'd all cheated her except Vassi. With him (perhaps) it had been love.

She lay on the bed through the night, never sleeping. She seldom slept now for more than a few minutes: and only then with Koos watching her. She'd done herself harm in her sleep, mutilating herself without knowing it, waking up bleeding and screaming with every limb sprouting needles she'd made out of her own skin and muscle, like a flesh cactus.

It was dark again, she guessed, but it was difficult to be sure. In this heavily curtained, bare-bulb lit room, it was a perpetual day to the senses, perpetual night to the soul. She would lie, bed-sores on her back, on her buttocks, listening to the far sounds of the street, sometimes dozing for a while, sometimes eating from Koos' hand, being washed, being toileted, being used.

A key turned in the lock. She strained from the mattress to see who it was. The door was opening . . . opening . . . opened.

Vassi. Oh God, it was Vassi at last, she could see him crossing the room towards her.

Let this not be another memory, she prayed, please let it be him this time: true and real.

"Jacqueline."

He said the name of her flesh, the whole name.

"Jacqueline." It *was* him.

Behind him, Koos stared between her legs, fascinated by the dance of her labia.

"Koo . . ." she said, trying to smile.

"I brought him," he grinned at her, not looking away from her sex.

"A day," she whispered. "I waited a day, Koos. You made me wait—"

"What's a day to you?" he said, still grinning.

She didn't need the pimp any longer, not that he knew that. In his innocence he thought Vassi was just another man she'd seduced along the way; to be drained and discarded like the others. Koos believed he would be needed tomorrow; that's why he played this fatal game so artlessly.

"Lock the door," she suggested to him. "Stay if you like."

"Stay?" he said, leering. "You mean, and watch?"

He watched anyway. She knew he watched through that hole he had bored in the door; she could hear him pant sometimes. But this time, let him stay forever.

Carefully, he took the key from the outside of the door, closed it, slipped the key into the inside and locked it. Even as the lock clicked she killed him, before he could even turn round and look at her again. Nothing spectacular in the execution; she just reached into his pigeon chest and crushed his lungs. He slumped against the door and slid down, smearing his face across the wood.

Vassi didn't even turn round to see him die; she was all he ever wanted to look at again.

He approached the mattress, crouched, and began to untie her ankles. The skin was chafed, the rope scabby with old blood. He worked at the knots systematically, finding a calm he thought he'd lost, a simple contentment in being here at the end, unable to go back, and knowing that the path ahead was deep in her.

When her ankles were free, he began on her wrists, interrupting her view of the ceiling as he bent over her. His voice was soft.

"Why did you let him do this to you?"

"I was afraid."

"Of what?"

"To move; even to live. Every day, agony."

"Yes."

He understood so well that total incapacity to exist.

She felt him at her side, undressing, then laying a kiss

on the sallow skin of the stomach of the body she occupied. It was marked with her workings; the skin had been stretched beyond its tolerance and was permanently criss-crossed.

He lay down beside her, and the feel of his body against hers was not unpleasant.

She touched his head. Her joints were stiff, the movements painful, but she wanted to draw his face up to hers. He came, smiling, into her sight, and they exchanged kisses.

My God, she thought, we are together.

And thinking they were together, her will was made flesh. Under his lips her features dissolved, becoming the red sea he'd dreamt of, and washing up over his face, that was itself dissolving: common waters made of thought and bone.

Her keen breasts pricked him like arrows; his erection, sharpened by her thought, killed her in return with his only thrust. Tangled in a wash of love they thought themselves extinguished, and were.

Outside, the hard world mourned on, the chatter of buyers and sellers continuing through the night. Eventually indifference and fatigue claimed even the eagerest merchant. Inside and out there was a healing silence: an end to losses and to gains.

THE SKINS OF THE FATHERS

The car coughed, and choked, and died. Davidson was suddenly aware of the wind on the desert road, as it keened at the windows of his Mustang. He tried to revive the engine, but it refused life. Exasperated, Davidson let his sweating hands drop off the wheel and surveyed the territory. In every direction, hot air, hot rock, hot sand. This was Arizona.

He opened the door and stepped out on to the baking dust highway. In front and behind it stretched unswervingly to the pale horizon. If he narrowed his eyes he could just make out the mountains, but as soon as he attempted to fix his focus they were eaten up by the heat-haze. Already the sun was corroding the top of his head, where his blond hair was thinning. He threw up the hood of the car and peered hopelessly into the engine, regretting his lack of mechanical know-how. Jesus, he thought, why don't they make the damn things fool-proof?

Then he heard the music.

It was so far off it sounded like a whistling in his ears at first: but it became louder.

It was music, of a sort.

How did it sound? Like the wind through telephone

lines, a sourceless, rhythmless, heartless air-wave plucking at the hairs on the back of his neck and telling them
to stand. He tried to ignore it, but it wouldn't go away.

He looked up out of the shade of the bonnet to find
the players, but the road was empty in both directions.
Only as he scanned the desert to the south-east did a line
of tiny figures become visible to him, walking, or skipping, or dancing at the furtherest edge of his sight, liquid in the heat off the earth. The procession, if that was
its nature, was long, and making its way across the desert parallel to the highway. Their paths would not cross.

Davidson glanced down once more into the cooling
entrails of his vehicle and then up again at the distant
line of dancers.

He needed help: no doubt of it.

He started off across the desert towards them.

Once off the highway the dust, not impacted by the
passage of cars, was loose: it flung itself up at his face
with every step. Progress was slow: he broke into a trot:
but they were receding from him. He began to run.

Over the thunder of his blood, he could hear the
music more loudly now. There was no melody apparent,
but a constant rising and falling of many instruments;
howls and hummings, whistlings, drummings and roar-
ings.

The head of the procession had now disappeared,
received into distance, but the celebrants (if that they
were) still paraded past. He changed direction a little, to
head them off, glancing over his shoulder briefly to
check his way back. With a stomach-churning sense of
loneliness he saw his vehicle, as small as a beetle on the
road behind him, sitting weighed down by a boiling sky.

He ran on. A quarter of an hour, perhaps, and he began to see the procession more clearly, though its leaders
were well out of sight. It was, he began to believe, a car-
nival of some sort, extraordinary as that seemed out
here in the middle of God's nowhere. The last dancers in
the parade were definitely costumed, however. They

wore headdresses and masks that tottered well above human height—there was the flutter of brightly-colored feathers, and streamers coiling in the air behind them. Whatever the reason for the celebration they reeled like drunkards, loping one moment, leaping the next, squirming, some of them, on the ground, bellies to the hot sand.

Davidson's lungs were torn with exhaustion, and it was clear he was losing the pursuit. Having gained on the procession, it was now moving off faster than he had strength or willpower to follow.

He stopped, bracing his arms on his knees to support his aching torso, and looked under his sweat-sodden brow at his disappearing salvation. Then, summoning up all the energy he could muster, he yelled:

Stop!

At first there was no response. Then, through the slits of his eyes, he thought he saw one or two of the revellers halt. He straightened up. Yes, one or two were looking at him. He felt, rather than saw, their eyes upon him.

He began to walk towards them.

Some of the instruments had died away, as though word of his presence was spreading among them. They'd definitely seen him, no doubt of that.

He walked on, faster now, and out of the haze, the details of the procession began to come clear.

His pace slowed a little. His heart, already pounding with exertion, thudded in his chest.

—My Jesus, he said, and for the first time in his thirty-six godless years the words were a true prayer.

He stood off half a mile from them, but there was no mistaking what he saw. His aching eyes knew papiermâché from flesh, illusion from misshapen reality.

The creatures at the end of the procession, the least of the least, the hangers-on, were monsters whose appearance beggared the nightmares of insanity.

One was perhaps eighteen or twenty feet tall. Its skin, that hung in folds on its muscle, was a sheath of spikes,

its head a cone of exposed teeth, set in scarlet gums.
Another was three-winged, its triple ended tail thrashing
the dust with reptilian enthusiasm. A third and fourth
were married together in a union of monstrosities the
result of which was more disgusting than the sum of its
parts. Through its length and breadth this symbiotic
horror was locked in seeping marriage, its limbs thrust
in and through wounds in its partner's flesh. Though the
tongues of its heads were wound together it managed a
cacophonous howl.

Davidson took a step back, and glanced round at the
car and the highway. As he did so one of the things,
black and red, began to scream like a whistle. Even at a
half mile's distance the noise cut into Davidson's head.
He looked back at the procession.

The whistling monster had left its place in the parade,
and its clawed feet were pounding the desert as it began to race towards him. Uncontrollable panic swept
through Davidson, and he felt his trousers fill as his
bowels failed him.

The thing was rushing towards him with the speed of
a cheetah, growing with every second, so he could see
more detail of its alien anatomy with every step. The
thumbless hands with their toothed palms, the head that
bore only a tri-colored eye, the sinew of its shoulder and
chest, even its genitals, erect with anger, or (God help
me) lust, two-pronged and beating against its abdomen.

Davidson shrieked a shriek that was almost the equal
of the monster's noise, and fled back the way he had
come.

The car was a mile, two miles away, and he knew it
offered no protection were he to reach it before the
monster overcame him. In that moment he realized how
close death was, how close it had always been, and he
longed for a moment's comprehension of this idiot horror.

It was already close behind him as his shit-slimed legs

buckled, and he fell, and crawled, and dragged himself towards the car. As he heard the thud of its feet at his back he instinctively huddled into a ball of whimpering flesh, and awaited the coup de grace.

He waited two heart-beats.

Three. Four. Still it didn't come.

The whistling voice had grown to an unbearable pitch, and was now fading a little. The gnashing palms did not connect with his body. Cautiously, expecting his head to be snapped from his neck at any moment, he peered through his fingers.

The creature had overtaken him.

Perhaps contemptuous of his frailty it had run on past him towards the highway.

Davidson smelt his excrement, and his fear. He felt curiously ignored. Behind him the parade had moved on. Only one or two inquisitive monsters still looked over their shoulders in his direction, as they receded into the dust.

The whistling now changed pitch. Davidson cautiously raised his head from ground level. The noise was all but outside his hearing-range, just a shrill whine at the back of his aching head.

He stood up.

The creature had leapt on to the top of his car. Its head was thrown back in a kind of ecstasy, its erection plainer than ever, the eye in its huge head glinting. With a final swoop to its voice, which took the whistle out of human hearing, it bent upon the car, smashing the windshield and curling its mouthed hands upon the roof. It then proceeded to tear the steel back like so much paper, its body twitching with glee, its head jerking about. Once the roof was torn up, it leapt on to the highway and threw the metal into the air. It turned in the sky and smashed down on the desert floor. Davidson briefly wondered what he could possibly put on the insurance form. Now the creature was tearing the vehicle apart. The doors were scattered. The engine was ripped out. The wheels slashed and wrenched off the axles.

To Davidson's nostrils there drifted the unmistakable stench of gasoline. No sooner had he registered the smell than a shard of metal glanced against another and the creature and the car were sheathed in a billowing column of fire, blackening into smoke as it balled over the highway.

The thing did not call out: or if it did its agonies were beyond hearing. It staggered out of the inferno with its flesh on fire, every inch of its body alight; its arms flailed wildly in a vain attempt to douse the fire, and it began to run off down the highway, fleeing from the source of its agony towards the mountains. Flames sprouted off its back and the air was tinged with the smell of its cooking flesh.

It didn't fall however, though the fire must have been devouring it. The run went on and on, until the heat dissolved the highway into the blue distance, and it was gone.

Davidson sank down on to his knees. The shit on his legs was already dry in the heat. The car continued to burn. The music had gone entirely, as had the procession.

It was the sun that drove him from the sand back towards his gutted car.

He was blank-eyed when the next vehicle along the highway stopped to pick him up.

Sheriff Josh Packard stared in disbelief at the claw prints on the ground at his feet. They were etched in slowly solidifying fat, the liquid flesh of the monster that had run through the main street (the only street) of Welcome minutes ago. It had then collapsed, breathing its last breath, and died in a writhing ball three trucks' length from the bank. The normal business of Welcome, the trading, the debating, the how do you do's had halted. One or two nauseous individuals had been received into the lobby of the Hotel while the smell of fricassied flesh thickened the good desert air of the town.

The stench was something between over-cooked fish and an exhumation, and it offended Packard. This was his town, overlooked by him, protected by him. The intrusion of this fireball was not looked upon kindly.

Packard took out his gun and began to walk towards the corpse. The flames were all but out now, having eaten the best of their meal. Even so destroyed by fire, it was a sizeable bulk. What might once have been its limbs were gathered around what might have been its head. The rest was beyond recognition. All in all, Packard was glad of that small mercy. But even in the charnel-house confusion of rendered flesh and blackened bone he could make out enough inhuman forms to quicken his pulse.

This was a monster: no doubt of it.

A creature from earth: out of earth, indeed. Up from the underworld and on its way to the great bowl for a night of celebration. Once every generation or so, his father had told him, the desert spat out its demons and let them loose awhile. Being a child who thought for himself Packard had never believed the shit his father talked but was this not such a demon?

Whatever mischance had brought this burning monstrosity into his town to die, there was pleasure for Packard in the proof of their vulnerability. His father had never mentioned that possibility.

Half-smiling at the thought of mastering such foulness, Packard stepped up to the smoking corpse and kicked it. The crowd, still lingering in the safety of the doorways, cooed with admiration at his bravery. The half-smile spread across his face. That kick alone would be worth a night of drinks, perhaps even a woman.

The thing was belly up. With the dispassionate gaze of a professional demon-kicker, Packard scrutinized the tangle of limbs across the head. It was quite dead, that was obvious. He sheathed his gun and bent towards the corpse.

"Get a camera out here, Jedediah," he said impressing even himself.

His deputy ran off towards the office.

"What we need," he said, "is a picture of this here beauty."

Packard went down on his haunches and reached across to the blackened limbs of the thing. His gloves would be ruined, but it was worth the inconvenience for the good this gesture would be doing for his public image. He could almost feel the admiring looks as he touched the flesh, and began to shake a limb loose from the head of the monster.

The fire had welded the parts together, and he had to wrench the limb free. But it came, with a jellied sound, revealing the heat-withered eye on the face beneath.

He dropped the limb back where it had come with a look of disgust.

A beat.

Then the demon's arm was snaking up—suddenly—too suddenly for Packard to move, and in a moment sublime with terror the Sheriff saw the mouth open in the palm of its forefoot and close again around his own hand.

Whimpering he lost balance and sat in the fat, pulling away from the mouth, as his glove was chewed through, and the teeth connected with his hand, clipping off his fingers as the rasping maw drew digits, blood and stumps further into its gut.

Packard's bottom slid in the mess under him and he squirmed, howling now, to loose himself. It still had life in it, this thing from the underworld. Packard bellowed for mercy as he staggered to his feet, dragging the sordid bulk of the thing up off the ground as he did so.

A shot sounded, close to Packard's car. Fluids, blood

and pus spattered him as the limb was blown to smithereens at the shoulder, and the mouth loosed its grip on Packard. The wasted mass of devouring muscle fell to the ground, and Packard's hand, or what was left of it, was in the open air again. There were no fingers remaining on his right hand, and barely half a thumb; the shattered bone of his digits jutted awkwardly from a partially chewed palm.

Eleanor Kooker dropped the barrel of the shotgun she had just fired, and grunted with satisfaction.

"Your hand's gone," she said, with brutal simplicity.

Monsters, Packard remembered his father telling him, never die. He'd remembered too late, and now he'd sacrificed his hand, his drinking, sexing hand. A wave of nostalgia for lost years with those fingers washed over him, while dots burst into darkness before his eyes. The last thing he saw as a dead faint carried him to the ground was his dutiful deputy raising a camera to record the whole scene.

The shack at the back of the house was Lucy's refuge and always had been. When Eugene came back drunk from Welcome, or a sudden fury took him because the stew was cold, Lucy retired into the shack where she could weep in peace. There was no pity to be had in Lucy's life. None from Eugene certainly, and precious little time to pity herself.

Today, the old source of irritation had got Eugene into a rage:

The child.

The nurtured and carefully cultivated child of their love; named after the brother of Moses, Aaron, which meant "exalted one." A sweet boy. The prettiest boy in the whole territory; five years old and already as charming and polite as any East Coast Momma could wish to raise.

Aaron.

Lucy's pride and joy, a child fit to blow bubbles in a picture book, fit to dance, fit to charm the Devil himself.

That was Eugene's objection.

"That fucking child's no more a boy than you are," he said to Lucy. "He's not even a half-boy. He's only fit for putting in fancy shoes and selling perfume. Or a preacher, he's fit for a preacher."

He pointed a nail-bitten, crook-thumbed hand at the boy.

"You're a shame to your father."

Aaron met his father's stare.

"You hear me, boy?"

Eugene looked away. The boy's big eyes made him sick to his stomach, more like a dog's eyes than anything human.

"I want him out of this house."

"What's he done?"

"He doesn't need to do a thing. It's sufficient he's the way he is. They laugh at me, you know that? They laugh at me because of him."

"Nobody laughs at you, Eugene."

"Oh yes—"

"Not for the boy's sake."

"Huh?"

"If they laugh, they don't laugh at the boy. They laugh at you."

"Shut your mouth."

"They know what you are, Eugene. They see you clear, clear as I see you."

"I tell you, woman—"

"Sick as a dog in the street, talking about what you've seen and what you're scared of—"

He struck her as he had many times before. The blow drew blood, as similar blows had for five years, but though she reeled, her first thoughts were for the boy.

"Aaron," she said through the tears the pain had brought. "Come with me."

"You let the bastard alone." Eugene was trembling.

"Aaron."

The child stood between father and mother, not knowing which to obey. The look of confusion on his face brought Lucy's tears more copiously.

"Mama," said the child, very quietly. There was a grave look in his eyes, that went beyond confusion. Before Lucy could find a way to cool the situation, Eugene had hold of the boy by his hair and was dragging him closer.

"You listen to your father, boy."

"Yes—"

"Yes, sir, we say to our father, don't we? We say, yes, sir."

Aaron's face was thrust into the stinking crotch of his father's jeans.

"Yes, sir."

"He stays with me, woman. You're not taking him out into that fucking shack one more time. He stays with his father."

The skirmish was lost and Lucy knew it. If she pressed the point any further, she only put the child at further risk.

"If you harm him—"

"I'm his father, woman," Eugene grinned. "What, do you think I'd hurt my own flesh and blood?"

The boy was locked to his father's hips in a position that was scarcely short of obscene. But Lucy knew her husband: and he was close to an outburst that would be uncontrollable. She no longer cared for herself—she'd had her joys—but the boy was so vulnerable.

"Get out of our sight, woman, why don't you? The boy and I want to be alone, don't we?"

Eugene dragged Aaron's face from his crotch and sneered down at his pale face.

"Don't we?"

"Yes, Papa."

"Yes, Papa. Oh yes indeed, Papa."

Lucy left the house and retired into the cool darkness of the shack, where she prayed for Aaron, named after the brother of Moses. Aaron, whose name meant "exalted one"; she wondered how long he could survive the brutalities the future would provide.

The boy was stripped now. He stood white in front of his father. He wasn't afraid. The whipping that would be meted out to him would pain him, but this was not true fear.

"You're sickly, lad," said Eugene, running a huge hand over his son's abdomen. "Weak and sickly like a runty hog. If I was a farmer, and you were a hog, you know what I'd do?"

Again, he took the boy by the hair. The other hand, between the legs.

"You know what I'd do, boy?"

"No, Papa. What would you do?"

The scored hand slid up over Aaron's body while his father made a slitting sound.

"Why, I'd cut you up and feed you to the rest of the litter. Nothing a hog likes better to eat, than hog-meat. How'd you like that?"

"No, Papa."

"You wouldn't like that?"

"No thank you, Papa."

Eugene's face hardened.

"Well I'd like to see that, Aaron. I'd like to see what you'd do if I was to open you up and have a look inside you."

There was a new violence in his father's games, which Aaron couldn't understand: new threats, new intimacy. Uncomfortable as he was the boy knew the real fear was felt not by him but by his father; fear was Eugene's birthright, just as it was Aaron's to watch, and wait, and suffer, until the moment came. He knew (without understanding how or why), that he would be an instrument in the destruction of his father. Maybe more than an instrument.

Anger erupted in Eugene. He stared at the boy, his brown fists clenched so tight that the knuckles burned white. The boy was his ruin, somehow; he'd killed the good life they'd lived before he was born, as surely as if he'd shot his parents dead. Scarcely thinking of what he was doing, Eugene's hands closed around the back of the boy's frail neck.

Aaron made no sound.

"I could kill you, boy."

"Yes, sir."

"What do you say to that?"

"Nothing, sir."

"You should say thank you, sir."

"Why?"

"Why, boy? 'Cause this life's not worth what a hog can shit, and I'd be doing you a loving service, as a father should a son."

"Yes, sir."

In the shack behind the house Lucy had stopped crying. There was no purpose in it; and besides, something in the sky she could see through the holes in the roof had brought memories to her that wiped the tears away. A certain sky: pure blue, sheeny-clear. Eugene wouldn't harm the boy. He wouldn't dare, ever dare, harm that child. He knew what the boy was, though he'd never admit to it.

She remembered the day, six years ago now, when the sky had been sheened like today, and the air had been livid with the heat. Eugene and she had been just about as hot as the air, they hadn't taken their eyes off each other all day. He was stronger then: in his prime. A soaring, splendid man, his body made heavy with work, and his legs so hard they felt like rock when she ran her hands over them. She had been quite a looker herself; the best damn backside in Welcome, firm and downy; a divide so softly haired Eugene couldn't keep from kissing her, even there, in the secret place. He'd pleasure her all day and all night sometimes; in the house they were building, or out on the sand in the late afternoon. The desert made a fine bed, and they could lie uninterrupted beneath the wide sky.

That day six years ago the sky had darkened too soon; long before night was due. It had seemed to blacken in a moment, and the lovers were suddenly cold in their hurried nakedness. She had seen, over his shoulder, the shapes the sky had taken: the vast and monumental creatures that were watching them. He, in his passion, still worked at her, thrust to his root and out the length again as he knew she delighted in, 'til a hand the color of beets and the size of a man pinched his neck, and plucked him out of his wife's lap. She watched him lifted into the sky like a squirming jack-rabbit, spitting from two mouths, North and South, as he finished his thrusts on the air. Then his eyes opened for a moment, and he saw his wife twenty feet below him, still bare, still spread butterfly wide, with monsters on every side. Casually, without malice, they threw him away, out of their ring of admiration, and out of her sight.

She remembered so well the hour that followed, the embraces of the monsters. Not foul in any way, not gross or harmful, never less than loving. Even the machineries of reproduction that they pierced her with, one after the other, were not painful, though some were as large as Eugene's fisted arm, and hard as bone. How many of those strangers took her that afternoon—three, four, five? Mingling their semen in her body, fondly teasing joy from her with their patient thrusts. When they went away, and her skin was touched with sunlight again, she felt, though on reflection it seemed shameful, a loss; as though the zenith of her life was passed, and the rest of her days would be a cold ride down to death.

She had got up at last, and walked over to where Eugene was lying unconscious on the sand, one of his legs broken by the fall. She had kissed him, and then squatted to pass water. She hoped, and hope it was, that there would be fruit from the seed of that day's love, and it would be a keepsake of her joy.

In the house Eugene struck the boy. Aaron's nose bled, but he made no sound.

"Speak, boy."

"What shall I say?"

"Am I your father or not?"

"Yes, father."

"Liar!"

He struck again, without warning; this time the blow carried Aaron to the floor. As his small, uncalloused palms flattened against the kitchen tiles to raise himself he felt something through the floor. There was a music in the ground.

"Liar!" his father was saying still.

There would be more blows to come, the boy thought, more pain, more blood. But it was bearable; and the music was a promise, after a long wait, of an end to blows once and for all.

Davidson staggered into the main street of Welcome. It was the middle of the afternoon, he guessed (his watch had stopped, perhaps out of sympathy), but the town appeared to be empty, until his eye alighted on the dark, smoking mound in the middle of the street, a hundred yards from where he stood.

If such a thing had been possible, his blood would have run cold at the sight.

He recognized what that bundle of burned flesh had been, despite the distance, and his head spun with horror. It had all been real after all. He stumbled on a couple more steps, fighting the dizziness and losing, until he felt himself supported by strong arms, and heard, through a fuzz of head-noises, reassuring words being spoken to him. They made no sense, but at least they were soft and human: he could give up any pretense to consciousness. He fainted, but it seemed there was only a moment of respite before the world came back into view again, as odious as ever.

He had been carried inside and was lying on an uncomfortable sofa, a woman's face, that of Eleanor Kooker, staring down at him. She beamed as he came round.

"The man'll survive," she said, her voice like cabbage going through a grater.

She leaned further forward.

"You seen the thing, did you?"

Davidson nodded.

"Better give us the low-down."

A glass was thrust into his hand and Eleanor filled it generously with whisky.

"Drink," she demanded, "then tell us what you got to tell—"

He downed the whisky in two, and the glass was immediately refilled. He drank the second glass more slowly, and began to feel better.

The room was filled with people: it was as though all of Welcome was pressing into the Kooker front parlor. Quite an audience: but then it was quite a tale. Loosened by the whisky, he began to tell it as best he could, without embellishment, just letting the words come. In return Eleanor described the circumstances of Sheriff Packard's "accident" with the body of the car-wrecker. Packard was in the room, looking the worse for consoling whiskies and pain killers, his mutilated hand bound up so well it looked more like a club than a limb.

"It's not the only devil out there," said Packard when the stories were out.

"So's you say," said Eleanor, her quick eyes less than convinced.

"My Papa said so," Packard returned, staring down at his bandaged hand. "And I believe it, sure as Hell I believe it."

"Then we'd best do something about it."

"Like what?" posed a sour looking individual leaning against the mantelpiece. "What's to be done about the likes of a thing that eats automobiles?"

Eleanor straightened up and delivered a well-aimed sneer at the questioner.

"Well let's have the benefit of your wisdom, Lou," she said. "What do *you* think we should do?"

"I think we should lie low and let 'em pass."

"I'm no ostrich," said Eleanor, "but if you want to go bury your head, I'll lend you a spade, Lou. I'll even dig you the hole."

General laughter. The cynic, discomforted, fell silent and picked at his nails.

"We can't sit here and let them come running through," said Packard's deputy, between blowing bubbles with his gum.

"They were going towards the mountains," Davidson said. "Away from Welcome."

"So what's to stop them changing their goddam minds?" Eleanor countered. "Well?"

No answer. A few nods, a few headshakings.

"Jedediah," she said, "you're deputy—what do you think about this?"

The young man with the badge and the gum flushed a little, and plucked at his thin moustache. He obviously hadn't a clue.

"I see the picture," the woman snapped back before he could answer. "Clear as a bell. You're all too shit-scared to go poking them divils out their holes, that it?"

Murmurs of self-justification around the room, more headshaking.

"You're just planning to sit yourselves down and let the women folk be devoured."

A good word: devoured. So much more emotive than eaten. Eleanor paused for effect. Then she said darkly: "Or worse."

Worse than devoured? Pity sakes, what was worse than devoured?

"You're not going to be touched by no divils," said

Packard, getting up from his seat with some difficulty. He swayed on his feet as he addressed the room.

"We're going to have them shit-eaters and lynch 'em."

This rousing battle-cry left the males in the room unroused; the sheriff was low on credibility since his encounter in Main Street.

"Discretion's the better part of valor," Davidson murmured under his breath.

"That's so much horse-shit," said Eleanor.

Davidson shrugged and finished off the whisky in his glass. It was not re-filled. He reflected ruefully that he should be thankful he was still alive. But his work-schedule was in ruins. He had to get to a telephone and hire a car; if necessary have someone drive out to pick him up. The "divils," whatever they were, were not his problem. Perhaps he'd be interested to read a few column-inches on the subject in *Newsweek*, when he was back East and relaxing with Barbara; but now all he wanted to do was finish his business in Arizona and get home as soon as possible.

Packard, however, had other ideas.

"You're a witness," he said, pointing at Davidson, "and as Sheriff of this community I order you to stay in Welcome until you've answered to my satisfaction all inquiries I have to put to you."

The formal language sounded odd from his slobbish mouth.

"I've got business—" Davidson began.

"Then you just send a cable and cancel that business, Mr.-fancy-Davidson."

The man was scoring points off him, Davidson knew, bolstering his shattered reputation by taking pot-shots at the Easterner. Still, Packard was the law: there was nothing to be done about it. He nodded his assent with as much good grace as he could muster. There'd be time to lodge a formal complaint against this hick-town Mussolini when he was home, safe and sound. For now, better to send a cable, and let business go hang.

"So what's the plan?" Eleanor demanded of Packard.

The Sheriff puffed out his booze-brightened cheeks.

"We deal with the divils," he said.

"How?"

"Guns, woman."

"You'll need more than guns, if they're as big as he says they are—"

"They are—" said Davidson, "believe me, they are."

Packard sneered.

"We'll take the whole fucking arsenal," he said jerking his remaining thumb at Jedediah. "Go break out the heavy-duty weapons, boy. Anti-tank stuff. Bazookas."

General amazement.

"You got bazookas?" said Lou, the mantelpiece cynic.

Packard managed a leering smile.

"Military stuff," he said, "left over from the Big One."

Davidson sighed inwardly. The man was a psychotic, with his own little arsenal of out-of-date weapons, which were probably more lethal to the user than to the victim. They were all going to die. God help him, they were all going to die.

"You may have lost your fingers," said Eleanor Kooker, delighted by this show of bravado, "but you're the only man in this room, Josh Packard."

Packard beamed and rubbed his crotch absent-mindedly. Davidson couldn't take the atmosphere of hand-me-down machismo in the room any longer.

"Look," he piped up, "I've told you all I know. Why don't I just let you folks get on with it."

"You ain't leaving," said Packard, "if that's what you're rooting after."

"I'm just saying—"

"We know what you're saying, son, and I ain't listening. If I see you hitch up your britches to leave I'll string you up by your balls. If you've got any."

The bastard would try it too, thought Davidson, even if he only had one hand to do it with. Just go with the flow, he told himself, trying to stop his lip curling. If Packard went out to find the monsters and his damn bazooka backfired, that was his business. Let it be.

"There's a whole tribe of them," Lou was quietly pointing out. "According to this man. So how do we take out so many of them?"

"Strategy," said Packard.

"We don't know their positions."

"Surveillance," replied Packard.

"They could really fuck us up, Sheriff," Jedediah observed, picking a collapsed gum-bubble from his moustache.

"This is our territory," said Eleanor. "We got it: we keep it."

Jedediah nodded.

"Yes, ma," he said.

"Suppose they just disappeared? Suppose we can't find them no more?" Lou was arguing. "Couldn't we just let 'em go to ground?"

"Sure," said Packard. "And then we're left waiting around for them to come out again and devour the women folk."

"Maybe they mean no harm—" Lou replied.

Packard's reply was to raise his bandaged hand.

"They done me harm."

That was incontestable.

Packard continued, his voice hoarse with feeling.

"Shit, I want them come-bags so bad I'm going out there with or without help. But we've got to out-think them, out-maneuver them, so we don't get anybody hurt."

The man talks some sense, thought Davidson. Indeed, the whole room seemed impressed. Murmurs of approval all round; even from the mantelpiece.

Packard rounded on the deputy again.

"You get your ass moving, son. I want you to call up that bastard Crumb out of Caution and get his boys down here with every goddam gun and grenade they've got. And if he asks what for you tell him Sheriff Packard's declaring a State of Emergency, and I'm requisitioning every asshole weapon in fifty miles, and the man on the other end of it. Move it, son."

Now the room was positively glowing with admiration, and Packard knew it.

"We'll blow the fuckers apart," he said.

For a moment the rhetoric seemed to work its magic on Davidson, and he half-believed it might be possible; then he remembered the details of the procession, tails teeth and all, and his bravado sank without trace.

They came up to the house so quietly, not intending to creep, just so gentle with their tread nobody heard them.

Inside, Eugene's anger had subsided. He was sitting with his legs up on the table, an empty bottle of whisky in front of him. The silence in the room was so heavy it suffocated.

Aaron, his face puffed up with his father's blows, was sitting beside the window. He didn't need to look up to see them coming across the sand towards the house, their approach sounded in his veins. His bruised face wanted to light up with a smile of welcome, but he repressed the instinct and simply waited, slumped in beaten resignation, until they were almost upon the house. Only when their massive bodies blocked out the sunlight through the window did he stand up. The boy's movement woke Eugene from his trance.

"What is it, boy?"

The child had backed off from the window, and was standing in the middle of the room, sobbing quietly with anticipation. His tiny hands were spread like sun-rays, his fingers jittering and twitching in his excitement.

"What's wrong with the window, boy?"

Aaron heard one of his true father's voices eclipse
Eugene's mumblings. Like a dog eager to greet his master after a long separation, the boy ran to the door and
tried to claw it open. It was locked and bolted.

"What's that noise, boy?"

Eugene pushed his son aside and fumbled with the
key in the lock, while Aaron's father called to his child
through the door. His voice sounded like a rush of
water, counterpointed by soft, piping sighs. It was an
eager voice, a loving voice.

All at once, Eugene seemed to understand. He took
hold of the boy's hair and hauled him away from the
door.

Aaron squealed with pain.

"Papa!" he yelled.

Eugene took the cry as addressed to himself, but
Aaron's true father also heard the boy's voice. His answering call was threaded with piercing notes of concern.

Outside the house Lucy had heard the exchange of
voices. She came out of the protection of her shack,
knowing what she'd see against that sheening sky, but
no less dizzied by the monumental creatures that had
gathered on every side of the house. An anguish went
through her, remembering the lost joys of that day six
years previous. They were all there, the unforgettable
creatures, an incredible selection of forms—

Pyramidal heads on rose colored, classically propor-
tioned torsos, that umbrellaed into shifting skirts of lace
flesh. A headless silver beauty whose six mother of pearl
arms sprouted in a circle from around its purring, pul-
sating mouth. A creature like a ripple on a fast-running
stream, constant but moving, giving out a sweet and
even tone. Creatures too fantastic to be real, too real to
be disbelieved; angels of the hearth and threshold. One
had a head, moving back and forth on a gossamer neck,
like some preposterous weather-vane, blue as the early
night sky and shot with a dozen eyes like so many suns.

Another father, with a body like a fan, opening and closing in his excitement, his orange flesh flushing deeper as the boy's voice was heard again.

"Papa!"

At the door of the house stood the creature Lucy remembered with greatest affection; the one who had first touched her, first soothed her fears, first entered her, infinitely gentle. It was perhaps twenty feet tall when standing at its full height. Now it was bowed towards the door, its mighty, hairless head, like that of a bird painted by a schizophrenic, bent close to the house as it spoke to the child. It was naked, and its broad, dark back sweated as it crouched.

Inside the house, Eugene drew the boy close to him, as a shield.

"What do you know, boy?"

"Papa?"

"I said what do you know?"

"Papa!"

Jubilation was in Aaron's voice. The waiting was over.

The front of the house was smashed inwards. A limb like a flesh hook curled under the lintel and hauled the door from its hinges. Bricks flew up and showered down again; wood-splinters and dust filled the air. Where there had once been safe darkness, cataracts of sunlight now poured onto the dwarfed human figures in the ruins.

Eugene peered up through the veil of dust. The roof was being peeled back by giant hands, and there was sky where there had been beams. Towering on every side he saw the limbs, bodies and faces of impossible beasts. They were teasing the remaining walls down, destroying his house as casually as he would break a bottle. He let the boy slip from his grasp without realizing what he'd done.

Aaron ran towards the creature on the threshold.

"Papa!"

It scooped him up like a father meeting a child out of school, and its head was thrown back in a wave of ecstasy. A long, indescribable noise of joy was uttered out of its length and breadth. The hymn was taken up by the other creatures, mounting in celebration. Eugene covered his ears and fell to his knees. His nose had begun to bleed at the first notes of the monster's music, and his eyes were full of stinging tears. He wasn't frightened. He knew they were not capable of doing him harm. He cried because he had ignored this eventuality for six years, and now, with their mystery and their glory in front of him, he sobbed not to have had the courage to face them and know them. Now it was too late. They'd taken the boy by force, and reduced his house, and his life, to ruins. Indifferent to his agonies, they were leaving, singing their jubilation, his boy in their arms forever.

In the township of Welcome organization was the by-word of the day. Davidson could only watch with admiration the way these foolish, hardy people were attempting to confront impossible odds. He was strangely enervated by the spectacle; like watching settlers, in some movie, preparing to muster paltry weaponry and simple faith to meet the pagan violence of the savage. But, unlike the movie, Davidson knew defeat was pre-ordained. He'd seen these monsters: awe-inspiring. Whatever the rightness of the cause, the purity of the faith, the savages trampled the settlers underfoot fairly often. The defeats just make it into the movies.

Eugene's nose ceased to bleed after half an hour or so, but he didn't notice. He was dragging, pulling, cajoling Lucy towards Welcome. He wanted to hear no explanations from the slut, even though her voice was babbling ceaselessly. He could only hear the sound of the monsters' churning tones, and Aaron's repeated call of "Papa," that was answered by a house-wrecking limb.

Eugene knew he had been conspired against, though even in his most tortured imaginings he could not grasp the whole truth.

Aaron was mad, he knew that much. And somehow his wife, his ripe-bodied Lucy, who had been such a beauty and such a comfort, was instrumental in both the boy's insanity and his own grief.

She'd sold the boy: that was his half-formed belief. In some unspeakable way she had bargained with these things from the underworld, and had exchanged the life and sanity of his only son for some kind of gift. What had she gained, for this payment? Some trinket or other that she kept buried in her shack? My God, she would suffer for it. But before he made her suffer, before he wrenched her hair from its holes, and tarred her flashing breasts with pitch, she would confess. He'd make her confess; not to him but to the people of Welcome—the men and women who scoffed at his drunken ramblings, laughed when he wept into his beer. They would hear, from Lucy's own lips, the truth behind the nightmares he had endured, and learn, to their horror, that demons he talked about were real. Then he would be exonerated, utterly, and the town would take him back into its bosom asking for his forgiveness, while the feathered body of his bitch-wife swung from a telephone pole outside the town's limits.

They were two miles outside Welcome when Eugene stopped.

"Something's coming."

A cloud of dust, and at its swirling heart a multitude of burning eyes.

He feared the worst.

"My Christ!"

He loosed his wife. Were they coming to fetch her too? Yes, that was probably another part of the bargain she'd made.

"They've taken the town," he said. The air was full of their voices; it was too much to bear.

They were coming at him down the road in a whining horde, driving straight at him—Eugene turned to run, letting the slut go. They could have her, as long as they left him alone; Lucy was smiling in to the dust.

"It's Packard," she said.

Eugene glanced back along the road and narrowed his eyes. The cloud of divils was resolving itself. The eyes at its heart were headlights, the voices were sirens; there was an army of cars and motorcycles, led by Packard's howling vehicle, careering down the road from Welcome.

Eugene was confounded. What was this, a mass exodus?

Lucy, for the first time that glorious day, felt a twinge of doubt.

As it approached, the convoy slowed, and came to a halt; the dust settled, revealing the extent of Packard's kamikaze squad. There were about a dozen cars and half a dozen bikes, all of them loaded with police weapons. A smattering of Welcome citizens made up the army, among them Eleanor Kooker. An impressive array of mean-minded, well-armed people.

Packard leant out of his car, spat, and spoke.

"Got problems, Eugene?" he asked.

"I'm no fool, Packard," said Eugene.

"Not saying you are."

"I seen these things. Lucy'll tell you."

"I know you have, Eugene; I know you have. There's no denying that there's divils in them hills, sure as shit. What'd you think I've got this posse together for, if it ain't divils?"

Packard grinned across to Jedediah at the wheel.

"Sure as shit," he said again. "We're going to blow them all to Kingdom Come."

From the back of the car, Miss Kooker leaned out the window; she was smoking a cigar.

"Seems we owe you an apology, Gene," she said, offering an apology for a smile. He's still a sot, she thought; marrying that fat-bottomed whore was the death of him. What a waste of a man.

Eugene's face tightened with satisfaction.

"Seems you do."

"Get in one of them cars behind," said Packard, "you and Lucy both; and we'll fetch them out of their holes like snakes—"

"They've gone towards the hills," said Eugene.

"That so?"

"Took my boy. Threw my house down."

"Many of them?"

"Dozen or so."

"OK Eugene, you'd best get in with us." Packard ordered a cop out of the back. "You're going to be hot for them bastards, eh?"

Eugene turned to where Lucy had been standing.

"And I want her tried—" he said.

But Lucy was gone, running off across the desert: doll-sized already.

"She's headed off the road," said Eleanor. "She'll kill herself."

"Killing's too good for her," said Eugene, as he climbed into the car. "That woman's meaner than the Devil himself."

"How's that, Gene?"

"Sold my only son to Hell, that woman—"

Lucy was erased by the heat-haze.

"—to Hell."

"Then let her be," said Packard. "Hell'll take her back, sooner or later."

Lucy had known they wouldn't bother to follow her. From the moment she'd seen the car lights in the dust-cloud, seen the guns, and the helmets, she knew she had little place in the events ahead. At best, she would be a spectator. At worst, she'd die of heatstroke crossing the desert, and never know the upshot of the oncoming battle. She'd often mused about the existence of the creatures who were collectively Aaron's father. Where they lived, why they'd chosen, in their wisdom, to make love to her. She'd wondered also whether anyone else in Welcome had knowledge of them. How many human eyes, other than her own, had snatched glimpses of their secret anatomies, down the passage of years? And of course she'd wondered if there would one day come a reckoning time, a confrontation between one species and the other. Now it seemed to be here, without warning, and against the background of such a reckoning her life was as nothing.

Once the cars and bikes had disappeared out of sight, she doubled back, tracing her footmarks in the sand, 'til she met the road again. There was no way of regaining Aaron, she realized that. She had, in a sense, merely been a guardian of the child, though she'd borne him. He belonged, in some strange way, to the creatures that had married their seeds in her body to make him. Maybe she'd been a vessel for some experiment in fertility, and now the doctors had returned to examine the resulting child. Maybe they had simply taken him out of love. Whatever the reasons she only hoped she would see the outcome of the battle. Deep in her, in a place touched only by monsters, she hoped for their victory, even though many of the species she called her own would perish as a result.

In the foothills there hung a great silence. Aaron had been set down amongst the rocks, and they gathered around him eagerly to examine his clothes, his hair, his eyes, his smile.

It was towards evening, but Aaron didn't feel cold. The breaths of his fathers were warm, and smelt, he thought, like the interior of the General Supplies Emporium in Welcome, a mingling of toffee and hemp, fresh cheeses and iron. His skin was tawny in the light of the diminishing sun, and at his zenith stars were appearing.

He was not happier at his mother's nipple than in that ring of demons.

At the toe of the foothills Packard brought the convoy to a halt. Had he known who Napoleon Bonaparte was, no doubt he would have felt like that conqueror. Had he known that conqueror's life-story, he might have sensed that this was his Waterloo: but Josh Packard lived and died bereft of heroes.

He summoned his men from their cars and went amongst them, his mutilated hand tucked in his shirt for support. It was not the most encouraging parade in military history. There were more than a few white and sickly-pale faces amongst his soldiers, more than a few eyes that avoided his stare as he gave his orders.

"Men," he bawled.

(It occurred to both Kooker and Davidson that as sneak-attacks went this would not be amongst the quietest.)

"Men—we've arrived, we're organized, and we've got God on our side. We've got the best of the brutes already, understand?"

Silence; baleful looks; more sweat.

"I don't want to see one jack man of you turn your heel and run, 'cause if you do and I set my eyes on you, you'll crawl home with your backside shot to Hell!!"

Eleanor thought of applauding; but the speech wasn't over.

"And remember, men," here Packard's voice dropped to a conspiratorial whisper, "these divils took Eugene's boy Aaron not four hours past. Took him fairly off his mother's tit, while she was rocking him to sleep. They ain't nothing but savages, whatever they may look like. They don't give a mind to a mother, or a child, or nothing. So when you get up close to one you just think how you'd have felt if you'd been taken from your mother's tit—"

He liked the phrase "mother's tit." It said so much, so simply. Momma's tit had a good deal more power to move these men than her apple pie.

"You've nothing to fear but seeming less than men, men."

Good line to finish on.

"Get on with it."

He got back into the car. Someone down the line began to applaud, and the clapping was taken up by the rest of them. Packard's wide red face was cleft with a hard yellow smile.

"Wagon's roll!" he grinned, and the convoy moved off into the hills.

Aaron felt the air change. It wasn't that he was cold: the breaths that warmed him remained as embracing as ever. But there was nevertheless an alteration in the atmosphere: some kind of intrusion. Fascinated, he watched his fathers respond to the change: their substance glinting with new colors, graver, warier colors. One or two even lifted their heads as if to sniff the air.

Something was wrong. Something, someone, was coming to interfere with this night of festival, unplanned and uninvited. The demons knew the signs and they were not unprepared for the eventuality. Was it not inevitable that the heroes of Welcome would come after the boy? Didn't the men believe, in their pitiable way, that their species was born out of earth's necessity to know itself, nurtured from mammal to mammal until it blossomed as humanity?

Natural then to treat the fathers as the enemy, to root them out and try to destroy them. A tragedy really: when the only thought the fathers had was of unity through marriage, that their children should blunder in and spoil the celebration.

Still, men would be men. Maybe Aaron would be different, though perhaps he too would go back in time into the human world and forget what he was learning here. The creatures who were his fathers were also men's fathers; and the marriage of semen in Lucy's body was the same mix that made the first males. Women had always existed: they had lived, a species to themselves, with the demons. But they had wanted playmates: and together they had made men.

What an error, what a cataclysmic miscalculation. Within mere eons, the worst rooted out the best; the women were made slaves, the demons killed or driven underground, leaving only a few pockets of survivors to attempt again that first experiment, and make men, like Aaron, who would be wiser to their histories. Only by infiltrating humanity with new male children could the master race be made milder. That chance was slim enough, without the interference of more angry children, their fat white fists hot with guns.

Aaron scented Packard and his stepfather, and smelling them, knew them to be alien. After tonight they would be known dispassionately, like animals of a different species. It was the gorgeous array of demons around him he felt closest to, and he knew he would protect them, if necessary, with his life.

Packard's car led the attack. The wave of vehicles appeared out of the darkness, their sirens blaring, their headlights on, and drove straight towards the knot of celebrants. From one or two of the cars terrified cops let out spontaneous howls of terror when the full spectacle came into view, but by that time the attack force was committed. Shots were fired. Aaron felt his fathers close around him protectively, their flesh now darkening with anger and fear.

Packard knew instinctively that these things were capable of fear, he could smell it off them. It was part of his job to recognize fear, to play on it, to use it against the miscreant. He screeched his orders into his microphone and led the cars into the circle of demons. In the back of one of the following cars Davidson closed his eyes and offered up a prayer to Yahweh, Buddha and Groucho Marx. Grant me power, grant me indifference, grant me a sense of humor. But nothing came to assist him: his bladder still bubbled, and his throat still throbbed.

Ahead, the shriek of brakes. Davidson opened his eyes (just a slit) and caught sight of one of the creatures wrapping its purple-black arm around Packard's car and lifting it into the air. One of the back doors flung open and a figure he recognized as Eleanor Kooker fell the few feet to the ground followed closely by Eugene. Leaderless, the cars were in a frenzy of collisions—the whole scene partially eclipsed by smoke and dust. There was the sound of breaking windscreens as cops took the quick way out of their cars; the shrieks of crumpling hoods and sheared off doors. The dying howl of a crushed siren; the dying plea of a crushed cop.

Packard's voice was clear enough, however, howling orders from his car even as it was lifted higher into the air, its engine revving, its wheels spinning foolishly in space. The demon was shaking the car as a child might a toy until the driver's door opened and Jedediah fell to the ground at the creature's skirt of skin. Davidson saw the skirt envelop the broken-backed deputy and appear to suck him into its folds. He could see too how Eleanor was standing up to the towering demon as it devoured her son.

"Jedediah, come out of there!" she shrieked, and fired shot after shot into his devourer's featureless, cylindrical head.

Davidson got out of the car to see better. Across a clutter of crashed vehicles and blood-spattered hoods he could make the whole scene out more plainly. The demons were sloping away from the battle, leaving this one extraordinary monster to hold the bridgehead. Quietly Davidson offered up a prayer of thanks to any passing deity. The divils were disappearing. There'd be no pitched battle: no hand-to-tentacle fight. The boy would be simply eaten alive, or whatever they planned for the poor little bastard. Indeed, couldn't he see Aaron from where he stood? Wasn't that his frail form the retreating demons were holding so high, like a trophy?

With Eleanor's curses and accusations in their ears the sheltering cops began to emerge from their hiding-places to surround the remaining demon. There was, after all, only one left to face, and it had their Napoleon in its slimy grip. They let off volley upon volley into its creases and tucks, and against the impartial geometry of its head, but the divil seemed unconcerned. Only when it had shaken Packard's car until the Sheriff rattled like a dead frog in a tin can did it lose interest and drop the vehicle. A smell of gasoline filled the air, and turned Davidson's stomach.

Then a cry: "Heads down!"

A grenade? Surely not; not with so much gasoline on the—

Davidson fell to the ground. A sudden silence, in which an injured man could be heard whimpering some-where in the chaos, then the dull, earth-rocking thud of the erupting grenade.

Somebody said Jesus Christ—with a kind of victory in his voice.

Jesus Christ. In the name of . . . for the glory of . . .

The demon was ablaze. The thin tissue of its gasoline-soaked skirt was burning; one of its limbs had been blown off by the blast, another partially destroyed; thick, colorless blood splashed from the wounds and the stump. There was a smell in the air like burnt candy: the creature was clearly in an agony of cremation. Its body reeled and shuddered as the flames licked up to ignite its empty face, and it stumbled away from its tormentors, not sounding its pain. Davidson got a kick out of seeing it burn: like the simple pleasure he had from putting the heel of his boot in the center of a jelly-fish. Favorite summer-time occupation of his childhood. In Maine: hot afternoons: spiking men-o'-war.

Packard was being dragged out of the wreckage of

his car. My God, that man was made of steel: he was standing upright and calling his men to advance on the enemy. Even in his finest hour, a flake of fire dropped from the flowering demon, and touched the lake of gasoline Packard was standing in. A moment later he, the car, and two of his saviors were enveloped in a billowing cloud of white fire. They stood no chance of survival: the flames just washed them away. Davidson could see their dark forms being wasted in the heart of the inferno, wrapped in folds of fire, curling in on themselves as they perished.

Almost before Packard's body had hit the ground Davidson could hear Eugene's voice over the flames.

"See what they've done? See what they've done?"

The accusation was greeted by feral howls from the cops.

"Waste them!" Eugene was screaming. "Waste them!"

Lucy could hear the noise of the battle, but she made no attempt to go in the direction of the foothills. Something about the way the moon was suspended in the sky, and the smell on the breeze, had taken all desire to move out of her. Exhausted, and enchanted, she stood in the open desert, and watched the sky.

When, after an age, she brought her gaze back down to fix on the horizon, she saw two things that were of mild interest. Out of the hills, a dirty smudge of smoke, and the edge of her vision in the gentle night light, a line of creatures, hurrying away from the hills. She suddenly began to run.

It occurred to her, as she ran, that her gait was sprightly as a young girl's, and that she had a young girl's motive: that is, she was in pursuit of her lover.

In an empty stretch of desert, the convocation of demons simply disappeared from sight. From where Lucy was standing, panting in the middle of nowhere, they seemed to have been swallowed up by the earth. She broke into a run again. Surely she could see her son and his fathers once more before they left forever? Or was she, after all her years of anticipation, to be denied even that?

In the lead car Davidson was driving, commandeered to do so by Eugene, who was not at present a man to be argued with. Something about the way he carried his rifle suggested he'd shoot first and ask questions later; his orders to the straggling army that followed him were two parts incoherent obscenities to one part sense. His eyes gleamed with hysteria: his mouth dribbled a little. He was a wild man, and he terrified Davidson. But it was too late now to turn back: he was in cahoots with the man for this last, apocalyptic pursuit.

"See, them black-eyed sons of bitches don't have no fucking heads," Eugene was screaming over the tortured roar of the engine. "Why you taking this track so slow, boy?"

He jabbed the rifle in Davidson's crotch.

"Drive, or I'll blow your brains out."

"I don't know which way they've gone," Davidson yelled back at Eugene.

"What you mean? Show me!"

"I can't show you if they've disappeared."

Eugene just about appreciated the sense of the response.

"Slow down, boy." He waved out of the car window to slow the rest of the army.

"Stop the car—stop the car!"

Davidson brought the car to a halt.

"And put those fucking lights out. All of you!"

The headlights were quenched. Behind, the rest of the entourage followed suit.

A sudden dark. A sudden silence. There was nothing to be seen or heard in any direction. They'd disappeared, the whole cacophonous tribe of demons had simply vanished into the air, chimerical.

The desert vista brightened as their eyes became accustomed to the gleam of the moonlight. Eugene got out of the car, rifle still at the ready, and stared at the sand, willing it to explain.

"Fuckers," he said, very softly.

Lucy had stopped running. Now she was walking towards the line of cars. It was all over by now. They had all been tricked: the disappearing act was a trump card no-one could have anticipated.

Then, she heard Aaron.

She couldn't see him, but his voice was as clear as a bell; and like a bell, it summoned. Like a bell, it rang out: this is a time of festival: celebrate with us.

Eugene heard it too; he smiled. They were near after all.

"Hey!" the boy's voice said.

"Where is he? You see him, Davidson?"

Davidson shook his head. Then—

"Wait! Wait! I see a light—look, straight ahead awhile."

"I see it."

With exaggerated caution, Eugene motioned Davidson back into the driver's seat.

"Drive, boy. But slowly. And no lights."

Davidson nodded. More jelly-fish for the spiking, he thought; they were going to get the bastards after all, and wasn't that worth a little risk? The convoy started up again, creeping forward at a snail's pace.

Lucy began to run once more: she could see the tiny figure of Aaron now, standing on the lip of a slope that led under the sand. The cars were moving towards it.

Seeing them approaching, Aaron stopped his calls and began to walk away, back down the slope. There was no need to wait any longer, they were following for certain. His naked feet made scarcely a mark in the soft-sanded incline that led away from the idiocies of the world. In the shadows of the earth at the end of that slope, fluttering and smiling at him, he could see his family.

"He's going in," said Davidson.

"Then follow the little bastard," said Eugene. "Maybe the kid doesn't know what he's doing. And get some light on him."

The headlights illuminated Aaron. His clothes were in tatters, and his body was slumped with exhaustion as he walked.

A few yards off to the right of the slope Lucy watched as the lead car drove over the lip of the earth and followed the boy down, into—

"No," she said to herself, "don't."

Davidson was suddenly scared. He began to slow the car.

"Get on with it, boy." Eugene jabbed the rifle into his crotch again. "We've got them cornered. We've got a whole nest of them here. The boy's leading us right to them."

The cars were all on the slope now, following the leader, their wheels slipping in the sand.

Aaron turned. Behind him, illuminated only by the phosphorescence of their own matter, the demons stood; a mass of impossible geometries. All the attributes of Lucifer were spread among the bodies of the fathers. The extraordinary anatomies, the dreaming spires of heads, the scales, the skirts, the claws, the clippers.

Eugene brought the convoy to a halt, got out of the car and began to walk towards Aaron.

"Thank you, boy," he said. "Come here—we'll look after you now. We've got them. You're safe."

Aaron stared at his father, uncomprehending.

The army was disgorging from the cars behind Eugene, readying their weapons. A bazooka was being hurriedly assembled; a cocking of rifles, a weighing-up of grenades.

"Come to Papa, boy," Eugene coaxed.

Aaron didn't move, so Eugene followed him a few yards deeper into the ground. Davidson was out of the car now, shaking from head to foot.

"Maybe you should put down the rifle. Maybe he's scared," he suggested.

Eugene grunted, and let the muzzle of the rifle drop a few inches.

"You're safe," said Davidson. "It's all right."

"Walk towards us, boy. Slowly."

Aaron's face began to flush. Even in the deceptive light of the headlamps it was clearly changing color. His cheeks were blowing up like balloons, and the skin on his forehead was wriggling as though his flesh was full of maggots. His head seemed to liquify, to become a soup of shapes, shifting and blossoming like a cloud, the façade of boyhood broken as the father inside the son showed its vast and unimaginable face.

Even as Aaron became his father's son, the slope began to soften. Davidson felt it first: a slight shift in the texture of the sand, as though an order had passed through it, subtle but all-pervasive.

Eugene could only gape as Aaron's transformation continued, his entire body now overtaken by the tremors of change. His belly had become distended and a harvest of cones budded from it, which even now flowered into dozens of coiled legs; the change was marvellous in its complexity, as out of the cradle of the boy's substance came new glories.

Without warning Eugene raised his rifle and fired at his son.

The bullet struck the boy-demon in the middle of his face. Aaron fell back, his transformation still taking its course even as his blood, a stream part scarlet, part silver, ran from his wound into the liquefying earth.

The geometries in the darkness moved out of hiding to help the child. The intricacy of their forms was simplified in the glare of the headlamps but they seemed, even as they appeared, to be changing again: bodies becoming thin in their grief, a whine of mourning like a solid wall of sound from their hearts.

Eugene raised his rifle a second time, whooping at his victory. He had them . . . My God, he had them. Dirty, stinking, faceless fuckers.

But the mud beneath his feet was like warm treacle as it rose around his shins, and when he fired he lost balance. He yelled for assistance, but Davidson was already staggering back up the slope out of the gully fighting a losing battle against the rising mire. The rest of the army were similarly trapped, as the desert liquified beneath them, and glutinous mud began to creep up the slope.

The demons had gone: retreated into the dark, their lament sunk away.

Eugene, flat on his back in the sinking sand, fired off two useless, vehement shots into the darkness beyond Aaron's corpse. He was kicking like a hog with its throat cut, and with every kick his body sunk deeper. As his face disappeared beneath the mud, he just glimpsed Lucy, standing at the edge of the slope, staring down towards Aaron's body. Then the mire covered his face, and blotted him out.

The desert was upon them with lightning speed.

One or two of the cars were already entirely submerged, and the tide of sand climbing the slope was relentlessly catching up with the escapees. Feeble cries for assistance ended with choking silences as mouths were filled with desert; somebody was shooting at the ground in an hysterical attempt to dam the flow, but it reached up swiftly to snatch every last one of them. Eleanor Kooker wasn't to be let free: she struggled, cursing and pressing the thrashing body of a cop deeper into the sand in her frantic attempts to step out of the gully.

There were universal howls now, as panicking men groped and grasped at each other for support, desperately trying to keep their heads afloat in the sea of sand.

Davidson was buried up to his waist. The ground that

eddied about his lower half was hot and curiously in-
viting. The intimacy of its pressure had given him an
erection. A few yards behind him a cop was screaming
blue murder as the desert ate him up. Further still from
him he could see a face peering out from the seething
ground like a living mask thrown on the earth. There
was an arm close by, still waving, as it sank; a pair of fat
buttocks was poking up from the silt sea like two water-
melons, a policeman's farewell.

Lucy took one step backwards as the mud slightly
overran the lip of the gully, but it didn't reach her feet.
Nor, curiously, did it dissipate itself, as a water-wave
might have done.

Like concrete, it hardened, fixing its living trophies
like flies in amber. From the lips of every face that still
took air came a fresh cry of terror, as they felt the desert
floor stiffen around their struggling limbs.

Davidson saw Eleanor Kooker, buried to breast-level.
Tears were pouring down her cheeks; she was sobbing
like a little girl. He scarcely thought of himself. Of the
East, of Barbara, of the children, he thought not at all.

The men whose faces were buried but whose limbs,
or parts of bodies, still broke surface, were dead of as-
phyxiation by now. Only Eleanor Kooker, Davidson
and two other men survived. One was locked in the
earth up to his chin, Eleanor was buried so that her
breasts sat on the ground, her arms were free to beat
uselessly at the ground that held her fast. Davidson
himself was held from his hips down. And most horribly, one pathetic victim was seen only by his nose and
mouth. His head was tipped back into the ground,
blinded by rock. Still he breathed, still he screamed.

Eleanor Kooker was scrabbling at the ground with
torn nails, but this was not loose sand. It was immov-
able.

"Get help," she demanded of Lucy, hands bleeding.

The two women stared at each other.

"Jesus God!" screamed the Mouth.

The Head was silent: by his glazed look it was apparent that he'd lost his mind.

"Please help us . . ." pleaded Davidson's Torso. "Fetch help."

Lucy nodded.

"Go!" demanded Eleanor Kooker. "Go!"

Numbly, Lucy obeyed. Already there was a glimmer of dawn in the east. The air would soon be blistering. In Welcome, three hours walk away, she would find only old men, hysterical women and children. She would have to summon help from perhaps fifty miles distance. Even assuming she found her way back. Even assuming she didn't collapse exhausted to the sand and die.

It would be noon before she could fetch help to the woman, to the Torso, to the Head, to the Mouth. By that time the wilderness would have had the best of them. The sun would have boiled their brain-pans dry, snakes would have nested in their hair, the buzzards would have hooked out their helpless eyes.

She glanced round once more at their trivial forms, dwarfed by the bloody sweep of the dawn sky. Little dots and commas of human pain on a blank sheet of sand; she didn't care to think of the pen that wrote them there. That was for tomorrow.

After a while, she began to run.

NEW MURDERS IN
THE RUE MORGUE

Winter, Lewis decided, was no season for old men. The snow that lay five inches thick on the streets of Paris froze him to the marrow. What had been a joy to him as a child was now a curse. He hated it with all his heart; hated the snowballing children (squeals, howls, tears); hated, too, the young lovers, eager to be caught in a flurry together (squeals, kisses, tears). It was uncomfortable and tiresome, and he wished he was in Fort Lauderdale, where the sun would be shining.

But Catherine's telegram, though not explicit, had been urgent, and the ties of friendship between them had been unbroken for the best part of fifty years. He was here for her, and for her brother Phillipe. However thin his blood felt in this ice land, it was foolish to complain. He'd come at a summons from the past, and he would have come as swiftly, and as willingly, if Paris had been burning.

Besides, it was his mother's city. She'd been born on the Boulevard Diderot, back in a time when the city was untrammelled by free-thinking architects and social engineers. Now every time Lewis returned to Paris he steeled himself for another desecration. It was happening less of late, he'd noticed. The recession in Europe made governments less eager with their bulldozers. But still, year after year, more fine houses found themselves rubble. Whole streets sometimes, gone to ground.

Even the Rue Morgue.

There was, of course, some doubt as to whether that infamous street had ever existed in the first place, but as his years advanced Lewis had seen less and less purpose in distinguishing between fact and fiction. That great divide was for young men, who still had to deal with life. For the old (Lewis was 73), the distinction was academic. What did it matter what was true and what was false, what real and what invented? In his head all of it, the half-lies and the truths, were one continuum of personal history.

Maybe the Rue Morgue had existed, as it had been described in Edgar Allan Poe's immortal story; maybe it was pure invention. Whichever, the notorious street was no longer to be found on a map of Paris.

Perhaps Lewis was a little disappointed not to have found the Rue Morgue. After all, it was part of his heritage. If the stories he had been told as a young boy were correct, the events described in the *Murders in the Rue Morgue* had been narrated to Poe by Lewis' grandfather. It was his mother's pride that her father had met Poe, while travelling in America. Apparently his grandfather had been a globe-trotter, unhappy unless he visited a new town every week. And in the winter of 1835 he had been in Richmond, Virginia. It was a bitter winter, perhaps not unlike the one Lewis was presently suffering, and one night the grandfather had taken refuge in a bar in Richmond. There, with a blizzard raging outside, he had met a small, dark, melancholy young man called Eddie. He was something of a local celebrity apparently, having written a tale that had won a competition in the *Baltimore Saturday Visitor*. The tale was "MS found in a bottle" and the haunted young man was Edgar Allan Poe.

The two had spent the evening together, drinking,

and (this is how the story went, anyway) Poe had gently pumped Lewis' grandfather for stories of the bizarre, of the occult and of the morbid. The worldly-wise traveller was glad to oblige, pouring out believe-it-or-not fragments that the writer later turned into *The Mystery of Marie Roget* and *The Murders in the Rue Morgue*. In both those stories, peering out from between the atrocities, was the peculiar genius of C. Auguste Dupin.

C. Auguste Dupin. Poe's vision of the perfect detective: calm, rational and brilliantly perceptive. The narratives in which he appeared rapidly became well-known, and through them Dupin became a fictional celebrity, without anyone in America knowing that Dupin was a real person.

He was the brother of Lewis' grandfather. Lewis' great uncle was C. Auguste Dupin.

And his greatest case—the Murders in the Rue Morgue—they too were based on fact. The slaughters that occurred in the story had actually taken place. Two women had indeed been brutally killed in the Rue Morgue. They were, as Poe had written, Madame L'Espanaye and her daughter Mademoiselle Camille L'Espanaye. Both women of good reputation, who lived quiet and unsensational lives. So much more horrible then to find those lives so brutally cut short. The daughter's body had been thrust up the chimney; the body of the mother was discovered in the yard at the back of the house, her throat cut with such savagery that her head was all but sawn off. No apparent motive could be found for the murders, and the mystery further deepened when all the occupants of the house claimed to have heard the voice of the murderer speaking in a different language. The Frenchman was certain the voice had spoken Spanish, the Englishman had heard German, the Dutchman thought it was French. Dupin, in his investigations, noted that none of the witnesses actually spoke the language they claimed to have heard from the lips of the unseen murderer. He concluded that the language was no language at all, but the wordless voice of a wild beast.

An ape in fact, a monstrous orang-outang from the East Indian Islands. Its tawny hairs had been found in the grip of the slain Madame L'Espanaye. Only its strength and agility made the appalling fate of Mademoiselle L'Espanaye plausible. The beast had belonged to a Maltese sailor, had escaped, and run riot in the bloody apartment on the Rue Morgue.

That was the bones of the story.

Whether true or not the tale held a great romantic appeal for Lewis. He liked to think of his great uncle logically pacing his way through the mystery, undistressed by the hysteria and horror around him. He thought of that calm as essentially European; belonging to a lost age in which the light of reason was still valued, and the worst horror that could be conceived of was a beast with a cut-throat razor.

Now, as the twentieth century ground through its last quarter, there were far greater atrocities to be accounted for, all committed by human beings. The humble orang-outang had been investigated by anthropologists and found to be a solitary herbivore; quiet and philosophical. The true monsters were far less apparent, and far more powerful. Their weapons made razors look pitiful; their crimes were vast. In some ways Lewis was almost glad to be old and close to leaving the century to its own devices. Yes, the snow froze his marrow. Yes, to see a young girl with a face of a goddess uselessly stirred his desires. Yes, he felt like an observer now instead of a participator.

But it had not always been that way.

In 1937, in the very room at number eleven, Quai de Bourbon, where he now sat, there had been experience enough. Paris was still a pleasure-dome in those days, studiously ignoring rumors of war, and preserving, though at times the strain told, an air of sweet naiveté.

They had been careless then; in both senses of the word, living endless lives of perfect leisure.

It wasn't so of course. The lives had not been perfect, or endless. But for a time—a summer, a month, a day—it had seemed nothing in the world would change.

In half a decade Paris would burn, and its playful guilt, which was true innocence, would be soiled permanently. They had spent many days (and nights) in the apartment Lewis now occupied, wonderful times; when he thought of them his stomach seemed to ache with the loss.

His thoughts turned to more recent events. To his New York exhibition, in which his series of paintings chronicling the damnation of Europe had been a brilliant critical success. At the age of seventy-three Lewis Fox was a fêted man. Articles were being written in every art periodical. Admirers and buyers had sprung up like mushrooms overnight, eager to purchase his work, to talk with him, to touch his hand. All too late, of course. The agonies of creation were long over, and he'd put down his brushes for the last time five years ago. Now, when he was merely a spectator, his critical triumph seemed like a parody: he viewed the circus from a distance with something approaching distaste.

When the telegram had come from Paris, begging for his assistance, he had been more than pleased to slip away from the ring of imbeciles mouthing his praise.

Now he waited in the darkening apartment, watching the steady flow of cars across the Pont Louis-Phillipe, as tired Parisians began the trek home through the snow. Their horns blared; their engines coughed and growled; their yellow foglamps made a ribbon of light across the bridge.

Still Catherine didn't come.

The snow, which had held off for most of the day, was beginning to fall again, whispering against the window. The traffic flowed across the Seine, the Seine flowed under the traffic. Night fell. At last, he heard footsteps in the hall; exchanged whispers with the house-keeper.

It was Catherine. At last, it was Catherine.

He stood up and stared at the door, imagining it opening before it opened, imagining her in the doorway.

"Lewis, my darling—"

She smiled at him; a pale smile on a paler face. She looked older than he'd expected. How long was it since he'd seen her? Four years or five? Her fragrance was the same as she always wore: and it reassured Lewis with its permanence. He kissed her cold cheeks lightly.

"You look well," he lied.

"No I don't," she said. "If I look well it's an insult to Phillipe. How can I be well when he's in such trouble?"

Her manner was brisk, and forbidding, as always.

She was three years his senior, but she treated him as a teacher would a recalcitrant child. She always had: it was her way of being fond.

Greetings over, she sat down beside the window, staring out over the Seine. Small grey ice-floes floated under the bridge, rocking and revolving in the current. The water looked deadly, as though its bitterness could crush the breath out of you.

"What trouble is Phillipe in?"

"He's accused of—"

A tiny hesitation. A flicker of an eyelid.

"—murder."

Lewis wanted to laugh; the very thought was preposterous. Phillipe was sixty-nine years old, and as mild-mannered as a lamb.

"It's true, Lewis. I couldn't tell you by telegram, you understand. I had to say it myself. Murder. He's accused of murder."

"Who?"

"A girl, of course. One of his fancy women."

"He still gets around, does he?"

"We used to joke he'd die on a woman, remember?"

Lewis half-nodded.

"She was nineteen. Natalie Perec. Quite an educated girl, apparently. And lovely. Long red hair. You remember how Phillipe loved redheads?"

"Nineteen? He has nineteen year olds?"

She didn't reply. Lewis sat down, knowing his pacing of the room irritated her. In profile she was still beautiful, and the wash of yellow-blue through the window softened the lines on her face, magically erasing fifty years of living.

"Where is he?"

"They locked him up. They say he's dangerous. They say he could kill again."

Lewis shook his head. There was pain at his temples, which might go if he could only close his eyes.

"He needs to see you. Very badly."

But maybe sleep was just an escape. Here was something even he couldn't be a spectator to.

Phillipe Laborteaux stared at Lewis across the bare, scored table, his face weary and lost. They had greeted each other only with hand shakes; all other physical contact was strictly forbidden.

"I am in despair," he said. "She's dead. My Natalie is dead."

"Tell me what happened."

"I have a little apartment in Montmartre. In the Rue des Martyrs. Just a room really, to entertain friends. Catherine always keeps number 11 so neat, you know, a man can't spread himself out. Natalie used to spend a lot of time with me there: everyone in the house knew her. She was so good natured, so beautiful. She was studying to go into Medical School. Bright. And she loved me."

Phillipe was still handsome. In fact, as the fashion in looks came full circle his elegance, his almost dashing face, his unhurried charm were the order of the day. A breath of a lost age, perhaps.

"I went out on Sunday morning: to the patisserie.
And when I came back . . ."

The words failed him for a moment.

"Lewis . . ."

His eyes filled with tears of frustration. This was so
difficult for him his mouth refused to make the necessary sounds.

"Don't—" Lewis began.

"I want to tell you, Lewis. I want you to know, I
want you to see her as I saw her—so you know what
there is . . . there is . . . what there is in the world."

The tears ran down his face in two graceful rivulets.
He gripped Lewis' hand in his, so tightly it ached.

"She was covered in blood. In wounds. Skin torn off
. . . hair torn out. Her tongue was on the pillow, Lewis.
Imagine that. She'd bitten it off in her terror. It was just
lying on the pillow. And her eyes, all swimming in
blood, like she'd wept blood. She was the dearest thing
in all creation, Lewis. She was beautiful."

"No more."

"I want to die, Lewis."

"No."

"I don't want to live now. There's no point."

"They won't find you guilty."

"I don't care, Lewis. You must look after Catherine
now. I read about the exhibition—"

He almost smiled.

"—Wonderful for you. We always said, didn't we?
before the war, you'd be the one to be famous, I'd
be—"

The smile had gone.

"—notorious. They say terrible things about me now,
in the newspapers. An old man going with young girls,
you see, that doesn't make me very wholesome. They
probably think I lost my temper because I couldn't perform with her. That's what they think, I'm certain." He
lost his way, halted, began again. "You must look after
Catherine. She's got money, but no friends. She's too

cool, you see. Too hurt inside; and that makes people
wary of her. You have to stay with her.''

"I shall.''

"I know. I know. That's why I feel happy, really, to
just . . .''

"No, Phillipe.''

"Just die. There's nothing left for us, Lewis. The
world's too hard.''

Lewis thought of the snow, and the ice-floes, and saw
the sense in dying.

The officer in charge of the investigation was less than
helpful, though Lewis introduced himself as a relative
of the esteemed Detective Dupin. Lewis' contempt for
the shoddily-dressed weasel, sitting in his cluttered hole
of an office, made the interview crackle with suppressed
anger.

"Your friend,'' the Inspector said, picking at the raw
cuticle of his thumb, "is a murderer, Monsieur Fox. It is
as simple as that. The evidence is overwhelming.''

"I can't believe that.''

"Believe what you like to believe, that's your pre-
rogative. We have all the evidence we need to convict
Phillipe Laborteaux of murder in the first degree. It was
a cold-blooded killing and he will be punished to the full
extent of the law. This is my promise.''

"What evidence do you have against him?''

"Monsieur Fox; I am not beholden to you. What evidence we have is our business. Suffice it to say that no
other person was seen in the house during the time that
the accused claims he was at some fictional patisserie;
and as access to the room in which the deceased was
found is only possible by the stairs—''

"What about a window?''

"A plain wall: three flights up. Maybe an acrobat: an
acrobat might do it.''

"And the state of the body?''

The Inspector made a face. Disgust.

"Horrible. Skin and muscle stripped from the bone. All the spine exposed. Blood; much blood."

"Phillipe is seventy."

"So?"

"An old man would not be capable—"

"In other respects," the Inspector interrupted, "he seems to have been quite capable, *oui*? The lover, yes? The passionate lover: he was capable of that."

"And what motive would you claim he had?"

His mouth scalloped, his eyes rolled and he tapped his chest.

"*Le coeur humain*," he said, as if despairing of reason in affairs of the heart. "*Le coeur humain, quel mystère, n'est-ce pas*?" and exhaling the stench of his ulcer at Lewis, he proffered the open door.

"Merci, Monsieur Fox. I understand your confusion, *oui*? But you are wasting your time. A crime is a crime. It is real; not like your paintings."

He saw the surprise on Lewis' face.

"Oh, I am not so uncivilized as not to know your reputation, Monsieur Fox. But I ask you, make your fictions as best you can; that is your genius, *oui*? Mine; to investigate the truth."

Lewis couldn't bear the weasel's cant any longer.

"Truth?" he snapped back at the Inspector. "You wouldn't know the truth if you tripped over it."

The weasel looked as though he'd been slapped with a wet fish.

It was precious little satisfaction; but it made Lewis feel better for at least five minutes.

The house on the Rue des Martyrs was not in good condition, and Lewis could smell the damp as he climbed to the little room on the third floor. Doors opened as he passed, and inquiring whispers ushered him up the stairs, but nobody tried to stop him. The room where the atrocity had happened was locked. Frustrated, but not knowing how or why it would help Phillipe's case to see the interior of the room, he made his way back down the stairs and into the bitter air.

Catherine was back at the Quai de Bourbon. As soon as Lewis saw her he knew there was something new to hear. Her grey hair was loosed from the bun she favored wearing, and hung unbraided at her shoulders. Her face was a sickly yellow-grey by the lamplight. She shivered, even in the clogged air of the centrally-heated apartment.

"What's wrong?" he asked.

"I went to Phillipe's apartment."

"So did I. It was locked."

"I have the key: Phillipe's spare key. I just wanted to pick up a few clothes for him."

Lewis nodded.

"And?"

"Somebody else was there."

"Police?"

"No."

"Who?"

"I couldn't see. I don't know exactly. He was dressed in a big coat, scarf over his face. Hat. Gloves." She paused. Then, "He had a razor, Lewis."

"A razor?"

"An open razor, like a barber."

Something jangled in the back of Lewis Fox's mind. An open razor; a man dressed so well he couldn't be recognized.

"I was terrified."

"Did he hurt you?"

She shook her head.

"I screamed and he ran away."

"Didn't say anything to you?"

"No."

"Maybe a friend of Phillipe's?"

"I know Phillipe's friends."

"Then of the girl. A brother."

"Perhaps. But—"

"What?"

"There was something odd about him. He smelt of perfume, stank of it, and he walked with such mincing little steps, even though he was huge."

Lewis put his arm around her.

"Whoever it was, you scared them off. You just mustn't go back there. If we have to fetch clothes for Phillipe, I'll gladly go."

"Thank you. I feel a fool: he may have just stumbled in. Come to look at the murder-chamber. People do that, don't they? Out of some morbid fascination . . ."

"Tomorrow I'll speak to the Weasel."

"Weasel?"

"Inspector Marais. Have him search the place."

"Did you see Phillipe?"

"Yes."

"Is he well?"

Lewis said nothing for a long moment.

"He wants to die, Catherine. He's given up fighting already, before he goes to trial."

"But he didn't do anything."

"We can't prove that."

"You're always boasting about your ancestors. Your blessed Dupin. You prove it . . ."

"Where do I start?"

"Speak to some of his friends, Lewis. *Please*. Maybe the woman had enemies."

Jacques Solal stared at Lewis through his round-bellied spectacles, his irises huge and distorted through the glass. He was the worse for too much cognac.

"She hadn't got any enemies," he said, "not her. Oh maybe a few women jealous of her beauty . . ."

Lewis toyed with the wrapped cubes of sugar that had come with his coffee. Solal was as uninformative as he was drunk; but unlikely as it seemed Catherine had described the runt across the table as Phillipe's closest friend.

"Do you think Phillipe murdered her?"

Solal pursed his lips.

"Who knows?"

"What's your instinct?"

"Ah; he was my friend. If I knew who had killed her I
would say so."

It seemed to be the truth. Maybe the little man was
simply drowning his sorrows in cognac.

"He was a gentleman," Solal said, his eyes drifting
towards the street. Through the steamed glass of the
Brasserie window brave Parisians were struggling
through the fury of another blizzard, vainly attempting
to keep their dignity and their posture in the teeth of a
gale.

"A gentleman," he said again.

"And the girl?"

"She was beautiful, and he was in love with her. She
had other admirers, of course. A woman like her—"

"Jealous admirers?"

"Who knows?"

Again: who knows? The inquiry hung on the air like a
shrug. Who knows? Who knows? Lewis began to understand the Inspector's passion for truth. For the first
time in ten years perhaps a goal apppeared in his life; an
ambition to shoot this indifferent "who knows?" out of
the air. To discover what had happened in that room on
the Rue des Martyrs. Not an approximation, not a fic-
tionalized account, but the truth, the absolute, unques-
tionable truth.

"Do you remember if there were any particular men
who fancied her?" he asked.

Solal grinned. He only had two teeth in his lower jaw.

"Oh yes. There was one."

"Who?"

"I never knew his name. A big man: I saw him outside the house three or four times. Though to smell him
you'd have thought—"

He made an unmistakable face that implied he

thought the man was homosexual. The arched eyebrows
and the pursed lips made him look doubly ridiculous
behind the thick spectacles.

"He smelt?"

"Oh yes."

"Of what?"

"Perfume, Lewis. Perfume."

Somewhere in Paris there was man who had known
the girl Phillipe loved. Jealous rage had overcome him.
In fit of uncontrollable anger he had broken into
Phillipe's apartment and slaughtered the girl. It was as
clear as that.

Somewhere in Paris.

"Another cognac?"

Solal shook his head.

"Already I'm sick," he said.

Lewis called the waiter across, and as he did so his eye
alighted on a cluster of newspaper clippings pinned
behind the bar.

Solal followed his gaze.

"Phillipe: he liked the pictures," he said.

Lewis stood up.

"He came here, sometimes, to see them."

The cuttings were old, stained and fading. Some were
presumably of purely local interest. Accounts of a fireball seen in a nearby street. Another about a boy of two
burned to death in his cot. One concerned an escaped
puma; one, an unpublished manuscript by Rimbaud; a
third (accompanied by a photograph) detailed casualties
in a plane crash at Orleans airport. But there were other
cuttings too; some far older than others. Atrocities, bizarre murders, ritual rapes, an advertisement for "Fan-
tomas," another for Cocteau's "La Belle et La Bete."
And almost buried under this embarrassment of bizar-
reries, was a sepia photograph so absurd it could have
come from the hand of Max Ernst. A half-ring of well-
dressed gentlemen, many sporting the thick moustaches
popular in the eighteen-nineties, were grouped around

the vast, bleeding bulk of an ape, which was suspended by its feet from a lamppost. The faces in the picture bore expressions of mute pride; of absolute authority over the dead beast, which Lewis clearly recognized as a gorilla. Its inverted head had an almost noble-tilt in death. Its brow was deep and furrowed, its jaw, though shattered by a fearsome wound, was thinly bearded like that of a patrician, and its eyes, rolled back in its head, seemed full of concern for this merciless world. They reminded Lewis, those rolling eyes, of the Weasel in his hole, tapping his chest.

"*Le coeur humain.*"

Pitiful.

"What is that?" he asked the acne-ridden barman, pointing at the picture of the dead gorilla.

A shrug was the reply: indifferent to the fate of men and apes.

"Who knows?" said Solal at his back. "Who knows?"

It was not the ape of Poe's story, that was certain. That tale had been told in 1835, and the photograph was far more recent. Besides, the ape in the picture was a gorilla: clearly a gorilla.

Had history repeated itself? Had another ape, a different species but an ape nevertheless, been loosed on the streets of Paris at the turn of the century?

And if so, if the story of the ape could repeat itself once . . . why not twice?

As Lewis walked through the freezing night back to the apartment at the Quai de Bourbon, the imagined repetition of events became more attractive; and now further symmetry presented itself to him. Was it possible that he, the great nephew of C. Auguste Dupin, might become involved in another pursuit, not entirely dissimilar from the first?

The key to Phillipe's room at the Rue des Martyrs was icy in Lewis' hand, and though it was now well past midnight he couldn't help but turn off at the bridge and make his way up the Boulevard de Sebastopol, west on to Boulevard Bonne-Nouvelle, then north again towards the Place Pigalle. It was a long, exhausting trudge, but he felt in need of the cold air, to keep his head clear of emotionalism. It took him an hour and a half to reach the Rue des Martyrs.

It was Saturday night, and there was still a lot of noise in a number of the rooms. Lewis made his way up the two flights as quietly as he could, his presence masked by the din. The key turned easily, and the door swung open.

Street lights illuminated the room. The bed, which dominated the space, was bare. Presumably sheets and blankets had been taken away for forensic tests. The eruption of blood onto the mattress was a mulberry color in the gloom. Otherwise, there was no sign of the violence the room had witnessed.

Lewis reached for the lightswitch, and snapped it on. Nothing happened. He stepped deeply into the room and stared up at the light fixture. The bulb was shattered.

He half thought of retreating, of leaving the room to darkness, and returning in the morning when there were fewer shadows. But as he stood under the broken bulb his eyes began to pierce the gloom a little better, and he began to make out the shape of a large teak chest of drawers along the far wall. Surely it was a matter of a few minutes work to find a change of clothes for Phillipe. Otherwise he would have to return the next day; another long journey through the snow. Better to do it now, and save his bones.

The room was large, and had been left in chaos by the police. Lewis stumbled and cursed as he crossed to the chest of drawers, tripping over a fallen lamp, and a shattered vase. Downstairs the howls and shrieks of a well-advanced party drowned any noise he made. Was it an orgy or a fight? The noise could have been either.

He struggled with the top drawer of the teak chest, and eventually wrenched it open, ferreting in the depths for the bare essentials of Phillipe's comfort: a clean undershirt, a pair of socks, initialled handkerchiefs, beautifully pressed.

He sneezed. The chilly weather had thickened the catarrh on his chest and the mucus in his sinuses. A handkerchief was to hand, and he blew his nose, clearing his blocked nostrils. For the first time the smell of the room came to him.

One odor predominated, above the damp, and the stale vegetables. Perfume, the lingering scent of perfume.

He turned into the darkened room, hearing his bones creak, and his eyes fell on the shadow behind the bed. A huge shadow, a bulk that swelled as it rose into view.

It was, he saw at once, the razor-wielding stranger. He was here: in waiting.

Curiously, Lewis wasn't frightened.

"What are you doing?" he demanded, in a loud, strong voice.

As he emerged from his hiding place the face of the stranger came into the watery light from the street; a broad, flat-featured, flayed face. His eyes were deep-set, but without malice; and he was smiling, smiling generously, at Lewis.

"Who are you?" Lewis asked again.

The man shook his head; shook his body, in fact, his gloved hands gesturing around his mouth. Was he dumb? The shaking of the head was more violent now, as though he was about to have a fit.

"Are you all right?"

Suddenly, the shaking stopped, and to his surprise Lewis saw tears, large, syrupy tears well up in the stranger's eyes and roll down his rough cheeks and into the bush of his beard.

As if ashamed of his display of feelings, the man turned away from the light, making a thick noise of sobbing in his throat, and exited. Lewis followed, more curious about this stranger than nervous of his intentions.

"Wait!"

The man was already half-way down the first flight of stairs, nimble despite his build.

"Please wait, I want to talk to you," Lewis began down the stairs after him, but the pursuit was lost before it was started. Lewis' joints were stiff with age and the cold, and it was late. No time to be running after a much younger man, along a pavement made lethal with ice and snow. He chased the stranger as far as the door and then watched him run off down the street; his gait was mincing as Catherine had said. Almost a waddle, ridiculous in a man so big.

The smell of his perfume was already snatched away by the north-east wind. Breathless, Lewis climbed the stairs again, past the din of the party, to claim a set of clothes for Phillipe.

The next day Paris woke to a blizzard of unprecedented ferocity. The calls to Mass went unrequited, the hot Sunday croissants went unbought, the newspapers lay unread on the vendor's stalls. Few people had either the nerve or the motive to step outside into the howling gale. They sat by their fires, hugging their knees, and dreamt of spring.

Catherine wanted to go to the prison to visit Phillipe, but Lewis insisted that he go alone. It was not simply the cold weather that made him cautious on her behalf; he had difficult words to say to Phillipe, delicate questions to ask him. After the previous night's encounter in his room, he had no doubt that Phillipe had a rival, probably a murderous rival. The only way to save Phillipe's life, it seemed, was to trace the man. And if that meant delving into Phillipe's sexual arrangements, then so be it. But it wasn't a conversation he, or Phillipe, would have wanted to conduct in Catherine's presence.

The fresh clothes Lewis had brought were searched, then given to Phillipe, who took them with a nod of thanks.

"I went to the house last night to fetch these for you."

"Oh."

"There was somebody in the room already."

Phillipe's jaw muscle began to churn, as he ground his teeth together. He was avoiding Lewis' eyes.

"A big man, with a beard. Do you know him, or *of* him?"

"No."

"Phillipe—"

"*No!*"

"The same man attacked Catherine," Lewis said.

"What?" Phillipe had begun to tremble.

"With a razor."

"Attacked her?" Phillipe said. "Are you sure?"

"Or was going to."

"No! He would never have touched her. Never!"

"Who is it, Phillipe? Do you know?"

"Tell her not to go there again; please, Lewis—" His eyes implored. "Please, for God's sake tell her never to go there again. Will you do that? Or you. Not you either."

"Who is it?"

"*Tell her.*"

"I will. But you must tell me who this man is, Phillipe."

He shook his head, grinding his teeth together audibly now.

"You wouldn't understand, Lewis. I couldn't expect you to understand."

"Tell me; I want to help."

"Just let me die."

"*Who is he?*"

"Just let me die . . . I want to forget, why do you try to make me remember? I want to—"

He looked up again: his eyes were bloodshot, and red-rimmed from nights of tears. But now it seemed there were no more tears left in him; just an arid place where there had been an honest fear of death, a love of love, and an appetite for life. What met Lewis' eyes was a universal indifference: to continuation, to self-preservation, to feeling.

"She was a whore," he suddenly exclaimed. His hands were fists. Lewis had never seen Phillipe make a fist in his life. Now his nails bit into the soft flesh of his palm until blood began to flow.

"Whore," he said again, his voice too loud in the little cell.

"Keep your row down," snapped the guard.

"A whore!" This time Phillipe hissed the accusation through teeth exposed like those of an angry baboon.

Lewis could make no sense of the transformation.

"You began all this—" Phillipe said, looking straight at Lewis, meeting his eyes fully for the first time. It was a bitter accusation, though Lewis didn't understand its significance.

"Me?"

"With your stories. With your damn Dupin."

"Dupin?"

"It was all a lie: all stupid lies. Women, murder—"

"You mean the Rue Morgue story?"

"You were so proud of that, weren't you? All those silly lies. None of it was true."

"Yes it was."

"No. It never was, Lewis: it was a story, that's all. Dupin, the Rue Morgue, the murders . . ."

His voice trailed away, as though the next words were unsayable.

". . . the ape."

Those were the words: the apparently unspeakable was spoken as though each syllable had been cut from his throat.

". . . the ape."

"What about the ape?"

"There are beasts, Lewis. Some of them are pitiful; circus animals. They have no brains; they are born victims. Then there are others."

"What others?"

"*Natalie was a whore*!" he screamed again, his eyes big as saucers. He took hold of Lewis' lapels, and began to shake him. Everybody else in the little room turned to look at the two old men as they wrestled over the table. Convicts and their sweethearts grinned as Phillipe was dragged off his friend, his words descending into incoherence and obscenity as he thrashed in the warder's grip.

"Whore! Whore! Whore!" was all he could say as they hauled him back to his cell.

Catherine met Lewis at the door of her apartment. She was shaking and tearful. Beyond her, the room was wrecked.

She sobbed against his chest as he comforted her, but she was inconsolable. It was many years since he'd comforted a woman, and he'd lost the knack of it. He was embarrassed instead of soothing, and she knew it. She broke away from his embrace, happier untouched.

"He was here," she said.

He didn't need to ask who. The stranger, the tearful, razor-wielding stranger.

"What did he want?"

"He kept saying 'Phillipe' to me. Almost saying it; grunting it more than saying it: and when I didn't answer he just destroyed the furniture, the vases. He wasn't even looking for anything: he just wanted to make a mess."

It made her furious: the uselessness of the attack.

The apartment was in ruins. Lewis wandered through the fragments of porcelain and shredded fabric, shaking his head. In his mind a confusion of tearful faces: Catherine, Phillipe, the stranger. Everyone in his nar-

row world, it seemed, was hurt and broken. Everyone
was suffering; and yet the source, the heart of the suffering, was nowhere to be found.

Only Phillipe had pointed an accusing finger: at
Lewis himself.

"You began all this." Weren't those his words? "You
began all this."

But how?

Lewis stood at the window. Three of the small panes
had been cracked by flying debris, and a wind was in-
sinuating itself into the apartment, with frost in its
teeth. He looked across at the ice-thickened waters of
the Seine; then a movement caught his eye. His stomach
turned.

The full face of the stranger was turned up to the window, his expression wild. The clothes he had always
worn so impeccably were in disarray, and the look on
his face was of utter, utter despair, so pitiful as to be
almost tragic. Or rather, a performance of tragedy: an
actor's pain. Even as Lewis stared down at him the
stranger raised his arms to the window in a gesture that
seemed to beg either forgiveness or understanding, or
both.

Lewis backed away from the appeal. It was too much;
all too much. The next moment the stranger was walking across the courtyard away from the apartment. The
mincing walk had deteriorated into a rolling lope. Lewis
uttered a long, low moan of recognition as the ill-
dressed bulk disappeared from view.

"Lewis?"

It wasn't a man's walk, that roll, that swagger. It was
the gait of an upright beast who'd been taught to walk,
and now, without its master, was losing the trick of it.

It was an ape.

Oh God, oh God, it was an ape.

"I have to see Phillipe Laborteaux."

"I'm sorry, Monsieur; but prison visitors—"

"This is a matter of life and death, officer."

"Easily said, Monsieur."

Lewis risked a lie.

"His sister is dying. I beg you to have some compassion."

"Oh . . . well."

A little doubt. Lewis levered a little further.

"A few minutes only; to settle arrangements."

"Can't it wait until tomorrow?"

"She'll be dead by morning."

Lewis hated talking about Catherine in such a way, even for the purpose of this deception, but it was necessary; he had to see Phillipe. If his theory was correct, history might repeat itself before the night was out.

Phillipe had been woken from a sedated sleep. His eyes were circled with darkness.

"What do you want?"

Lewis didn't even attempt to proceed any further with his lie; Phillipe was drugged as it was, and probably confused. Best to confront him with the truth, and see what came of it.

"You kept an ape, didn't you?"

A look of terror crossed Phillipe's face, slowed by the drugs in his blood, but plain enough.

"Didn't you?"

"Lewis . . ." Phillipe looked so very old.

"Answer me, Phillipe, I beg you: before it's too late. Did you keep an ape?"

"It was an experiment, that's all it was. An experiment."

"Why?"

"Your stories. Your damn stories: I wanted to see if it was true that they were wild. I wanted to make a man of it."

"Make a man of it."

"And that whore . . ."

"Natalie."

"She seduced it."

Lewis felt sick. This was a convolution he hadn't anticipated.

"Seduced it?"

"Whore," Phillipe said, with infinite regret.

"Where is this ape of yours?"

"You'll kill it."

"It broke into the apartment, while Catherine was there. Destroyed everything, Phillipe. It's dangerous now that it has no master. Don't you understand?"

"Catherine?"

"No, she's all right."

"It's trained: it wouldn't harm her. It's watched her, in hiding. Come and gone. Quiet as a mouse."

"And the girl?"

"It was jealous."

"So it murdered her?"

"Perhaps. I don't know. I don't want to think about it."

"Why haven't you told them; had the thing destroyed?"

"I don't know if it's true. It's probably all a fiction, one of your damn fictions, just another story."

A sour, wily smile crossed his exhausted face.

"You must know what I mean, Lewis. It could be a story, couldn't it? Like your tales of Dupin. Except that maybe I made it true for a while; did you ever think of that? Maybe I made it true."

Lewis stood up. It was a tired debate: reality and illusion. Either a thing was, or was not. Life was not a dream.

"Where is the ape?" he demanded.

Phillipe pointed to his temple.

"Here; where you can never find him," he said, and spat in Lewis' face. The spittle hit his lip, like a kiss.

"You don't know what you did. You'll never know."

Lewis wiped his lip as the warders escorted the prisoner out of the room and back to his happy drugged oblivion. All he could think of now, left alone in the cold interview room, was that Phillipe had it easy. He'd taken refuge in pretended guilt, and locked himself away where memory, and revenge, and the truth, the wild, marauding truth, could never touch him again. He hated Phillipe at that moment, with all his heart. Hated him for the dilettante and the coward he'd always known him to be. It wasn't a more gentle world Phillipe had created around him; it was a hiding place, as much a lie as that summer of 1937 had been. No life could be lived the way he'd lived it without a reckoning coming sooner or later; and here it was.

That night, in the safety of his cell, Phillipe woke. It was warm, but he was cold. In the utter dark he chewed at his wrists until a pulse of blood bubbled into his mouth. He lay back on his bed, and quietly splashed and fountained away to death, out of sight and out of mind.

The suicide was reported in a small article on the second page of *Le Monde*. The big news of the following day however was the sensational murder of a redheaded prostitute in a little house off the Rue de Rochechquant. Monique Zevaco had been found at three o'clock in the morning by her flatmate, her body in a state so horrible as to "defy description."

Despite the alleged impossibility of the task, the media set about describing the indescribable with a morbid will. Every last scratch, tear and gouging on Monique's partially nude body—tattooed, drooled *Le Monde*, with a map of France—was chronicled in detail. As indeed was the appearance of her well-dressed, over-perfumed murderer, who had apparently watched her at her toilet through a small back window, then broken in and attacked Mademoiselle Zevaco in her bathroom. The murderer had then fled down the stairs, bumping into the flatmate who would minutes after discover Mademoiselle Zevaco's mutilated corpse. Only one commentator made any connection between the murder at the

Rue des Martyrs and the slaughter of Mme. Zevaco; and he failed to pick up on the curious coincidence that the accused Phillipe Laborteaux had that same night taken his own life.

The funeral took place in a storm, the cortège edging its pitiful way through the abandoned streets towards Montparnasse with the lashing snow entirely blotting out the road ahead. Lewis sat with Catherine and Jacques Solal as they laid Phillipe to rest. Every one of his circle had deserted him, unwilling to attend the funeral of a suicide and of a suspected murderer. His wit, his good looks, his infinite capacity to charm went for nothing at the end.

He was not, as it turned out, entirely unmourned by strangers. As they stood at the graveside, the cold cutting into them, Solal sidled up to Lewis and nudged him.

"What?"

"Over there. Under the tree." Solal nodded beyond the praying priest.

The stranger was standing at a distance, almost hidden by the marble mausoleums. A heavy black scarf was wrapped across his face, and a wide-brimmed hat pulled down over his brow, but his bulk was unmistakable. Catherine had seen him too. She was shaking as she stood, wrapped round by Lewis' embrace, not just with cold, but with fear. It was as though the creature was some morbid angel, come to hover a while, and enjoy the grief. It was grotesque, and eerie, that this thing should come to see Phillipe consigned to the frozen earth. What did it feel? Anguish? Guilt?

Yes, did it feel guilt?

It knew it had been seen, and it turned its back, shambling away. Without a word to Lewis, Jacques Solal slipped away from the grave in pursuit. In a short while both the stranger and his pursuer were erased by the snow.

Back at the Quai de Bourbon Catherine and Lewis said nothing of the incident. A kind of barrier had appeared between them, forbidding contact on any level but the most trivial. There was no purpose in analysis, and none in regrets. Phillipe was dead. The past, their past together, was dead. This final chapter in their joint lives soured utterly everything that preceded it, so that no shared memory could be enjoyed without the pleasure being spoilt. Phillipe had died horribly, devouring his own flesh and blood, perhaps driven mad by a knowledge he possessed of his own guilt and depravity. No innocence, no history of joy could remain unstained by that fact. Silently they mourned the loss, not only of Phillipe, but of their own past. Lewis understood now Phillipe's reluctance to live when there was such loss in the world.

Solal rang. Breathless after his chase, but elated, he spoke in whispers to Lewis, clearly enjoying the excitement.

"I'm at the Gare du Nord, and I've found out where our friend lives. I've found him, Lewis!"

"Excellent. I'll come take a cab: ten minutes."

"It's in the basement of number sixteen, Rue des Fleurs. I'll see you there—"

"Don't go in, Jacques. Wait for me. Don't—"

The telephone clicked and Solal was gone. Lewis reached for his coat.

"Who was that?"

She asked, but she didn't want to know. Lewis shrugged on his overcoat and said: "Nobody at all. Don't worry. I won't be long."

"Take your scarf," she said, not glancing over her shoulder.

"Yes. Thank you."

"You'll catch a chill."

He left her gazing over the night-clad Seine, watching the ice-floes dance together on the black water.

· · ·

When he arrived in the house on the Rue des Fleurs, Solal was not to be seen, but fresh footprints in the powdery snow led to the front door of number sixteen and then, foiled, went around the back of the house. Lewis followed them. As he stepped into the yard behind the house, through a rotted gate that had been crudely forced by Solal, he realized he had come without a weapon. Best to go back, perhaps, find a crowbar, a knife; something. Even as he was debating with himself, the back door opened, and the stranger appeared, dressed in his now familiar overcoat. Lewis flattened himself against the wall of the yard, where the shadows were deepest, certain that he would be seen. But the beast was about other business. He stood in the doorway with his face fully exposed, and for the first time, in the reflected moonlight off the snow, Lewis could see the creature's physiognomy plainly. Its face was freshly shaved; and the scent of cologne was strong, even in the open air. Its skin was pink as a peach, though nicked in one or two places by a careless blade. Lewis thought of the open-razor it had apparently threatened Catherine with. Was that what its business had been in Phillipe's room, the purloining of a good razor? It was pulling its leather gloves on over its wide, shaved hands, making small coughing noises in its throat that sounded almost like grunts of satisfaction. Lewis had the impression that it was preparing itself for the outside world; and the sight was touching as much as intimidating. All this thing wanted was to be human. It was aspiring, in its way, to the model Phillipe had given it, had nurtured in it. Now, deprived of its mentor, confused and unhappy, it was attempting to face the world as it had been taught to do. There was no way back for it. Its days of innocence had gone: it could never be an unambitious beast again. Trapped in its new persona, it had no choice but to continue in the life its master had awoken its taste for. Without glancing in Lewis' direction, it gently closed the door behind it and crossed the yard, its walk transforming in those few steps from a simian roll to the mincing waddle that it used to simulate humanity.

Then it was gone.

Lewis waited a moment in the shadows, breathing shallowly. Every bone in his body ached with cold now, and his feet were numb. The beast showed no sign of returning; so he ventured out of his hiding place and tried the door. It was not locked. As he stepped inside a stench struck him: the sickly sweet smell of rotten fruit mingled with the cloying cologne: the zoo and the boudoir.

He edged down a flight of slimy stone steps, and along a short, tiled corridor towards a door. It too was unlocked; and the bare bulb inside illuminated a bizarre scene.

On the floor, a large, somewhat thread-bare Persian carpet; sparse furnishings; a bed, roughly covered with blankets and stained hessian; a wardrobe, bulging with oversize clothes; discarded fruit in abundance, some trodden into the floor; a bucket, filled with straw and stinking of droppings. On the wall, a large crucifix. On the mantelpiece a photograph of Catherine, Lewis and Phillipe together in a sunlit past, smiling. At the sink, the creature's shaving kit. Soap, brush, razor. Fresh suds. On the dresser a pile of money, left in careless abundance beside a pile of hypodermics and a collection of small bottles. It was warm in the beast's garret; perhaps the furnace for the house roared in an adjacent cellar. Solal was not there.

Suddenly, a noise.

Lewis turned to the door, expecting the ape to be filling it, teeth bared, eyes demonic. But he had lost all orientation; the noise was not from the door but from the wardrobe. Behind the pile of clothes there was a movement.

"Solal?"

Jacques Solal half fell out of the wardrobe, and sprawled across the Persian carpet. His face was disfigured by one foul wound, so that it was all but impossible to find any part of his features that was still Jacques.

The creature had taken hold of his lip and pulled his muscle off his bone, as though removing a balaclava. His exposed teeth chattered away in nervous response to oncoming death; his limbs jangled and shook. But Jacques was already gone. These shudders and jerks were not signs of thought or personality, just the din of passing. Lewis knelt at Solal's side; his stomach was strong. During the war, being a conscientious objector, he had volunteered to serve in the Military Hospital, and there were few transformations of the human body he had not seen in one combination or another. Tenderly, he cradled the body, not noticing the blood. He hadn't loved this man, scarcely cared for him at all, but now all he wanted was to take him away, out of the ape's cage, and find him a human grave. He'd take the photograph too. That was too much, giving the beast a photograph of the three friends together. It made him hate Phillipe more than ever.

He hauled the body off the carpet. It required a gargantuan effort, and the sultry heat in the room, after the chill of the outside world, made him dizzy. He could feel a jittering nervousness in his limbs. His body was close to betraying him, he knew it; close to failing, to losing its coherence and collapsing.

Not here. In God's name, not here.

Maybe he should go now, and find a phone. That would be wise. Call the police, yes . . . call Catherine, yes . . . even find somebody in the house to help him. But that would mean leaving Jacques in the lair, for the beast to assault again, and he had become strangely protective of the corpse; he was unwilling to leave it alone. In an anguish of confused feelings, unable to leave Jacques yet unable to move him far, he stood in the middle of the room and did nothing at all. That was best; yes. Nothing at all. Too tired, too weak. Nothing at all was best.

The reverie went on interminably; the old man fixed beyond movement at the crux of his feelings, unable to go forward into the future, or back into the soiled past. Unable to remember. Unable to forget.

Waiting, in a dreamy half-life, for the end of the world.

It came home noisily like a drunken man, and the sound of its opening the outer door stirred Lewis into a slow response. With some difficulty he hauled Jacques into the wardrobe, and hid there himself, with the faceless head in his lap.

There was a voice in the room, a woman's voice. Maybe it wasn't the beast, after all. But no: through the crack of the wardrobe door Lewis could see the beast, and a red-haired young woman with him. She was talking incessantly, the perpetual trivia of a spaced-out mind.

"You've got more; oh you sweetie, oh you dear man, that's wonderful. Look at all this stuff."

She had pills in her hands and was swallowing them like sweets, gleeful as a child at Christmas.

"Where did you get all this? OK, if you don't want to tell me, its fine by me."

Was this Phillipe's doing too, or had the ape stolen the stuff for his own purposes? Did he regularly seduce redheaded prostitutes with drugs?

The girl's grating babble was calming now, as the pills took effect, sedating her, transporting her to a private world. Lewis watched, entranced, as she began to undress.

"It's so . . . hot . . . in here."

The ape watched, his back to Lewis. What expression did that shaved face wear? Was there lust in its eyes, or doubt?

The girl's breasts were beautiful, though her body

was rather too thin. The young skin was white, the nipples flower-pink. She raised her arms over her head and as she stretched the perfect globes rose and flattened slightly. The ape reached a wide hand to her body and tenderly plucked at one of her nipples, rolling it between dark-meat fingers. The girl sighed.

"Shall I . . . take everything off?"

The monkey grunted.

"You don't say much, do you?"

She shimmied out of her red skirt. Now she was naked but for a pair of knickers. She lay on the bed stretching again, luxuriating in her body and the welcome heat of the room, not even bothering to look at her admirer.

Wedged underneath Solal's body, Lewis began to feel dizzy again. His lower limbs were not completely numb, and he had no feeling in his right arm, which was pressed against the back of the wardrobe, yet he didn't dare move. The ape was capable of anything, he knew that. If he was discovered what might it not choose to do, to him and to the girl?

Every part of his body was now either nerveless, or wracked with pain. In his lap Solal's seeping body seemed to become heavier with every moment. His spine was screaming, and the back of his neck pained him as though pierced with hot knitting-needles. The agony was becoming unbearable; he began to think he would die in this pathetic hiding place, while the ape made love.

The girl sighed, and Lewis looked again at the bed. The ape had its hand between her legs, and she squirmed beneath its ministrations.

"Yes, oh yes," she said again and again, as her lover stripped her completely.

It was too much. The dizziness throbbed through Lewis' cortex. Was this death? The lights in the head, and the whine in the ears?

He closed his eyes, blotting out the sight of the lovers,

but unable to shut out the noise. It seemed to go on forever, invading his head. Sighs, laughter, little shrieks.

At last, darkness.

Lewis woke on an invisible rack; his body had been wrenched out of shape by the limitations of his hiding-place. He looked up. The door of the wardrobe was open, and the ape was staring down at him, its mouth attempting a grin. It was naked; and its body was almost entirely shaved. In the cleft of its immense chest a small gold crucifix glinted. Lewis recognized the jewelry immediately. He had bought it for Phillipe in the Champs Elysees just before the war. Now it nestled in a tuft of reddish-orange hair. The beast proffered a hand to Lewis, and he automatically took it. The coarse-palmed grip hauled him from under Solal's body. He couldn't stand straight. His legs were rubbery, his ankles wouldn't support him. The beast took hold of him, and steadied him. His head spinning, Lewis looked down into the wardrobe, where Solal was lying, tucked up like a baby in its womb, face to the wall.

The beast closed the door on the corpse, and helped Lewis to the sink, where he was sick.

"Phillipe?" He dimly realized that the woman was still here: in the bed: just woken after a night of love.

"Phillipe: who's this?" She was scrabbling for pills on the table beside the bed. The beast sauntered across and snatched them from her hands.

"Ah . . . Phillipe . . . please. Do you want me to go with this one as well? I will if you want. Just give me back the pills."

She gestured towards Lewis.

"I don't usually go with old men."

The ape growled at her. The expression on her face changed, as though for the first time she had an inkling of what this john was. But the thought was too difficult for her drugged mind, and she let it go.

"Please, Phillipe . . ." she whimpered.

Lewis was looking at the ape. It had taken the photograph from the mantelpiece. Its dark nail was on Lewis' picture. It was smiling. It recognized him, even though forty-odd years had drained so much life from him.

"Lewis," it said, finding the word quite easy to say.

The old man had nothing in his stomach to vomit, and no harm left to feel. This was the end of the century, he should be ready for anything. Even to be greeted as a friend of a friend by the shaved beast that loomed in front of him. It would not harm him, he knew that. Probably Phillipe had told the ape about their lives together; made the creature love Catherine and himself as much as it had adored Phillipe.

"Lewis," it said again, and gestured to the woman, (now sitting open-legged on the bed) offering her for his pleasure.

Lewis shook his head.

In and out, in and out, part fiction, part fact.

It had come to this; offered a human woman by this naked ape. It was the last, God help him, the very last chapter in the fiction his great uncle had begun. From love to murder back to love again. The love of an ape for a man. He had caused it, with his dreams of fictional heroes, steeped in absolute reason. He had coaxed Phillipe into making real the stories of a lost youth. He *was* to blame. Not this poor strutting ape, lost between the jungle and the Stock Exchange; not Phillipe, wanting to be young forever; certainly not cold Catherine, who after tonight would be completely alone. It was him. His the crime, his the guilt, his the punishment.

His legs had regained a little feeling, and he began to stagger to the door.

"Aren't you staying?" said the red-haired woman.

"This thing . . ." he couldn't bring himself to name the animal.

"You mean Phillipe?"

"He isn't called Phillipe," Lewis said. "He's not even human."

"Please yourself," she said, and shrugged.

To his back, the ape spoke, saying his name. But this time, instead of it coming out as a sort of grunt-word, its simian palate caught Phillipe's inflexion with unnerving accuracy, better than the most skillful of parrots. It was Phillipe's voice, perfectly.

"Lewis," it said.

Not pleading. Not demanding. Simply naming, for the pleasure of naming, an equal.

The passers-by who saw the old man clamber on to the parapet of the Pont du Carrousel stared, but made no attempt to stop him jumping. He teetered a moment as he stood up straight, then pitched over into the threshing, churning ice-water.

One or two people wandered to the other side of the bridge to see if the current had caught him: it had. He rose to the surface, his face blue-white and blank as a baby's, then some intricate eddy snatched at his feet and pulled him under. The thick water closed over his head and churned on.

"Who was that?" somebody asked.

"Who knows?"

It was a clear-heaven day; the last of the winter's snow had fallen, and the thaw would begin by noon. Birds, exulting in the sudden sun, swooped over the Sacré Coeur. Paris began to undress for spring, its virgin white too spoiled to be worn for long.

In mid-morning, a young woman with red hair, her arm linked in that of a large ugly man, took a leisurely stroll to the steps of the Sacré Coeur. The sun blessed them. Bells rang.

It was a new day.